THE TEMPESTUOUS WOOING

To Lily, Frances & Hilda
Love From
Katrina Britt

How could Sheena reveal her love for the powerful and dangerous Ross Carlyle when he believed the tissue of lies her sister had told him about her, and despised her for what he knew her to be . . .?

Books you will enjoy
by KATRINA BRITT

THE MAN AT KEY WEST

Much as she loved her father, Sue Blake had always found it difficult to cope with his way of life—always jetting around the world, never at home for more than a few days. So when she met the forceful Jay Denver, whose lifestyle was indistinguishable from her father's, she was determined not to get involved with him . . .

SUCH MEN ARE DANGEROUS

After the glamour of her career as a model Sorella found the primitive hardships of Julian's plantation weakened her determination to make their marriage work. She loved him so much, but could she be so selfish as to keep him from the woman he really loved . . .?

THAT MAN IS MINE

Ross Dyson was as ruthlessly determined in his passion as he was in his business and he wanted Lynn enough to go to any lengths to make her his. But what frightened Lynn more was the intensity of her own feelings for him . . .

THE TEMPESTUOUS WOOING

BY

KATRINA BRITT

MILLS & BOON LIMITED
15–16 BROOK'S MEWS
LONDON W1A 1DR

First published in Great Britain 1986
by Mills & Boon Limited

ISBN 0 263 11071 0

Set in Monophoto Times 10 on 11 pt.
07–0486 – 56676

Made and printed in Great Britain by
Richard Clay (The Chaucer Press) Ltd,
Bungay, Suffolk

CHAPTER ONE

SHEENA opened long-lashed violet eyes and luxuriantly stretched her shapely limbs. The beautifully furnished bedroom with its built-in furniture in white and gold and off-white wall to wall carpet was easy on the eyes. She sighed with pleasure. Her holiday in London was over and it had been fun. It was a pity it could not have lasted longer than a fortnight, but she had been lucky to have such an exciting holiday in pleasant surroundings. The holiday had been planned a long time ago when Dawn had returned from modelling in the States. The two girls with whom Dawn had shared an apartment were now both married and she was to end the lease in order to marry an American she had met in the States.

Sheena had been hurt when her sister had not invited her to the wedding, which was to take place in the States.

'There's no reason why you should go to all the expense of flying to the USA,' Dawn had argued philosophically. 'It isn't as if you had a career to come back to. You will need to take care of every penny until you get another job. It was hard luck that your firm folded up when it did, but that's just something you'll have to overcome and leave behind as a bad experience."

Sheena had flinched inwardly at her sister's outspokenness She had never expected the engineering firm where she had worked as a secretary to fail, but it had.

She slipped from between the sheets, found her wrap and padded to the bathroom. Turning on the bathtaps she reached for a jar of perfumed bathsalts and sprinkled some into the steaming water. After luxuriating for a blissful length of time, she stepped out of the perfumed water and used one of the thick fluffy towels. Once dry, she put on beige slacks and a green sleeveless top, fixed a matching green band around her thick, auburn hair and made for the kitchen.

There was no welcoming aroma of freshly-made coffee which meant that Dawn was not yet up. Not that Sheena expected her to be at eight o'clock in the morning. Her sister never went to work before ten. In any case she had been out the previous evening to a party and had arrived back home in the small hours.

Sheena finished her breakfast and was making fresh coffee in order to take a cup to her sister when she heard the front door open and close. Before she could conjecture on who it might be, Dawn appeared in the doorway.

'Dawn!' Sheena almost shrieked in her surprise as wide-eyed she took in her sister's midnight blue evening dress. The shade was one that flattered blondes, not that Dawn needed anything flattering to make her look good. She had a gift for giving flair to anything she wore. She stood in the doorway with an air of practised languor, breathing in the pleasant scent of the percolating coffee. 'Have you been out all night?' Sheena asked weakly.

Dawn daintily stifled a yawn behind well-manicured pink nails, and replied languidly, 'I'm afraid so. It was a most depressing party.' She patted her silver blonde hair and turned to leave the room. 'Bring me a drink while I relax in my room. I'm worn to a frazzle.'

When Sheena entered the room with a tray of steaming coffee, Dawn was in bed in a cobweb-fine silk negligé, resting on a mound of pillows. After carefully placing the tray across her sister's knees, Sheena sat down on the bed. 'If it was such a dull party how come you stayed out all night?' she asked curiously.

Dawn sipped her coffee. 'It's a little hard to explain. You see there was this absolutely gorgeous man . . . he hit me like a thunderbolt. Oh! It's all so unfair.' She put the cup down and looked despairingly at Sheena, putting out a hand in a hopeless gesture of pleading. 'Here is this dishy man and I'm almost married to someone else.'

'You can't have your cake and eat it,' Sheena said drily. 'If you have found out that you've made a mistake about your fiancé then don't get married.'

'It isn't as simple as that. After all I've only just met Ross and I don't know if he feels the same way about me as I feel about him. He is kind of enigmatic. You know the kind of man I mean—all male and arrogant with it. He's so good-looking and he's exciting. What's more he makes one feel so special.'

Sheena shook her head dazedly. 'All this in one evening! He certainly made an impression on you. Did you go to bed with him?'

Dawn laughed, then her eyes suddenly went dreamy. 'Of course not, but don't think I could have said no to him if he had suggested it.'

Sheena took a deep breath. Coming from Dawn, who was always so level-headed this revelation was shattering. Dawn had never been the emotional type and like her sister she had never slept around. Sheena had always regarded Dawn as a cool type of person. It was the first time that her sister had confessed to going overboard for any man.

'Tell me more,' she insisted. 'What is this Adonis like? What makes him so good-looking? Is he rugged or smooth and sculptured? What is it about this disturbing member of the opposite sex that has knocked you for six? Is he young?'

'About thirty.' If Dawn had sagged before with tiredness she was now very much alive as she described the man. 'He looks like the archetypal gipsy—dark hair all crispy curly, dark flashing eyes and the most wicked smile. He is rather tall, wide shouldered, slim hipped and terrifically fit. He moves with the grace of a panther.' The silver-grey eyes sparkled at the memory and she hugged her shoulders as though aching for his arms.

Sheena said matter-of-factly, 'Your coffee is getting cold. While we are on the subject of men, though, where does this leave your Frank? Are you still going to marry him?'

Dawn sipped her coffee. 'I suppose so. If only I could have a little more time, though.' She looked disgruntled and not at all like a happy bride to be. 'If I thought that Ross was serious about me, I would tell Frank that I've changed my mind.'

'You've changed your mind before about marrying. I am sure you can do it again, but if you do, I want no part of it. Frank is a very nice man and he can give you everything you desire. Is this Ross person English?'

'Yes, he's well-educated, but not as wealthy as Frank, of course.'

Sheena's lip curled. 'I never thought I would see the time when you let your heart rule your head. I thought I was the romantic one, not you.'

Dawn put down her empty cup and lifted slender lace-clad shoulders. 'I probably had too much to drink last night, although my head feels clear enough so I can't have had that much. I should be all right—I have to be because we are giving a party here, this evening.'

Sheena looked at her sharply. 'Are you sure you'll feel up to it? I'm going back today or have you forgotten about that?'

Dawn put a hand to her head. 'Oh, Lord! I had

forgotten. You don't have to hurry back, though, do you? You can stay until I leave for the States, can't you?'

Sheena surveyed the high-cheekboned face, the grey eyes returning her regard almost pleadingly. She loved Dawn in spite of her shortcomings. Dawn would not have become such a successful model if Sheena had not paid the fees for the modelling school. They had both been at school when the aunt who had brought them up had died, leaving them with very little. Sheena, the elder by two years, had taken a secretarial course on leaving boarding school in order to earn enough money to set Dawn off on the career she had longed for.

Everything had gone well for the first six months until Dawn had gone abroad during her training, on a modelling job, and had picked up some bug which laid her low for well over two years. It had been touch and go for a long while as to whether or not she would eventually recover, but she did. Sheena had nursed her devotedly as well as holding down her own job. All her money had gone on Dawn and her needs. Until a year ago she had been paying the last instalments on a bill for Dawn's convalescence which had been taken at a place in Switzerland.

'I suppose I can,' she said slowly, wishing silently that her sister was not quite so selfish. She had been earning a large salary and commanding high fees for quite a while now, but it had virtually all been spent on clothes and make-up—two essential ingredients in making the best of the modelling business. Sheena had not asked for help in paying off old bills. She had been only too thankful that Dawn had recovered so completely—besides which, Dawn had never offered.

This matter of another man on what was virtually the eve of her sister's wedding, disturbed Sheena far more deeply than bills and finance. She liked Frank Manders and his air of dependability. He was a big, fair-haired man with the shoulders of an American football player. He was charming and well-mannered and Sheena liked his selfless concern for others. He came from a well-known Boston family and she knew that Dawn would have every chance of happiness with him. She liked Massachusetts and would settle down there happily. Their ages were fairly compatible too. Dawn was twenty-two, Frank, twenty-eight, and in the real-estate business.

Sheena at twenty-four already felt quite jaded. Maybe losing her job had something to do with it.

The arrangements for the party that evening were left mostly to her. Dawn slept for several hours, drank lots of black coffee on awakening and went through her extensive wardrobe of clothes like a tornado, throwing out expensive dresses and suits at random. Sheena, going into her room to tell her that lunch was ready, stared in dismay at the piles of clothes scattered untidily on the carpet.

'You aren't throwing all this lot out, surely?' she gasped. 'Aren't you being a little drastic?'

Dawn turned from the wardrobe in the act of throwing out a beautiful, pure-silk suit in the colour of *crème de menthe*.

She said peevishly, 'I am only doing what I do every year, throwing out most of my wardrobe so that I can restock it.'

Sheena said quietly, 'Well, it's all right for some. Lunch is ready. When we've eaten we can go over the arrangements for this evening. I'll have to do some shopping, but you won't want to stock up on food if you're going to be leaving in two days' time.'

Dawn looked thoughtful. 'No, we won't, will we? I do hope the party goes well tonight. Thank goodness you can cook and bake!'

The telephone beside Dawn's bed buzzed and Dawn looked warily at her sister before she calmly picked up the receiver.

'Don't forget that lunch is ready,' Sheena whispered urgently, before leaving the room.

Dawn had looked rather flushed on sitting down to lunch. Sheena made no comment upon it, however. It was none of her business, but she felt an upsurge of worry as she watched Dawn plough through her prawn salad.

She said, 'Will it be the usual crowd this evening for your grand farewell spree? I've made adequate amounts of everything in case we run short.'

Dawn shrugged carelessly, 'I suppose there will be the usual last minute arrivals.' She put her empty plate to one side and reached for the coffee. 'I'm very grateful for your help. I shall have to see about having you over for a holiday with Frank and me when we are settled. Perhaps by that time you will be married yourself. Coffee?'

She reached over to fill her own cup.

Sheena smiled, 'I'll see how your marriage works out first. In the meantime, though, I have to get a job.'

Dawn put down the coffee pot and added sugar to her cup.

'Why not look over the men who come to the party this evening? Some of them are good husband material and they liked you,' she said lightly. 'But I forgot. You're the romantic kind who has to fall in love first.' She raised her coffee to her lips. 'You are old-fashioned, Sheena. It just doesn't happen like that anymore.'

Sheena popped the last piece of lettuce into her mouth and reached for the coffee. When she had poured herself a cupful she said tolerantly, 'The men who came to our last party enjoyed my cooking and I enjoyed watching them enjoying it, that's all. I kept one or two of the dates I made but there was nothing serious. As for falling in love, I happen to think that it is essential to know that you can bear sharing everything, including your body, with a man before committing oneself.'

'So?'

'I would say that a certain amount of feeling between partners is essential for when the newness wears off and the nitty-gritty beneath the initial novelty and mystery is revealed. Otherwise it has no meaning. One can't find out about total compatibility just by sleeping together.'

Dawn drank her coffee. 'Well, don't look at me. Thank goodness I haven't got such an all-or-nothing attitude. I mean to keep my figure intact.'

'You mean no children?'

'Exactly.'

'But is that fair on Frank?'

Dawn gestured with expressive hands as if to prove that she was being fair to her intended. 'He wants me, doesn't he? There are no strings attached that I know of. I shall keep him perfectly happy.'

'You don't really love him, do you?' Sheena asked sadly.

Dawn's smile held tolerance and a little pathos. 'I'm very fond of him and I wouldn't hurt him for anything. Now, I must dash.'

'Not to work surely? After all you leave tomorrow night for Boston.'

'I want to buy a few clothes—including a dress for this evening.'

'But . . .' Whatever Sheena was going to say faded into thin air for Dawn had gone, leaving her sister with visions of the heaps of discarded suits and dresses in her room.

Later, picking up the discarded clothing and folding

everything neatly, Sheena allowed her thoughts to dwell on her sister. Her one wish was for her to be happy in her marriage. Once she was settled, she might change her mind about having children. Dawn's a lucky girl, she thought, then broke away from her dreaming to hurry in her task in order to get back to the kitchen and complete the preparations for the party that evening.

The party was going well. Sheena had met most of the guests who had come to say farewell to Dawn. The camera team, the models, their escorts and other friends of her sister including various dates she had had. Dawn was circulating, resplendent in her new dress—though Sheena still could not understand why she had bought it. A mantle patterned with delicately shaded pink clouds was charmingly set off by a swirling underskirt in white. A whisper of silver on Dawn's eyelids gave her eyes an extra grey gleam of beauty. Her silvery blonde hair was a shining cap framing her animated face.

As Sheena wove her way between huddles of guests with refreshments, she could not help but notice the number of times Dawn cast her gaze to the door of the room, as if she was expecting someone. Sheena was on the far side of the room having gone to fetch more refreshments when from the corner of her eye she caught Dawn's sudden movement. She had moved towards the door to greet a newcomer and was tipping her blonde head back to meet his gaze.

Dawn was two inches taller than Sheena, who was of average height, but the man she was talking to was taller and bigger than most. He moved to stand before one of the wall lights and his dark crisp hair gleamed in its glow. His features were clear-cut and arresting, from the dark intelligent eyes, the arrogant blade of a nose to the firm jaw, mobile mouth and very white teeth. The latter contrasted startlingly with his deep tan and judging by the long brown fingers curled around the drink Dawn had procured for him, that tan covered his whole body. His dark suit fitted him impeccably well and his whole manner was one of consummate ease. His dark eyes gleamed wickedly as he said something to Dawn with a wry smile. His mouth twitched slightly as he voiced the mockery apparent in his expression.

Here, thought Sheena darkly, was a man not to be taken lightly. He was dangerous from the top of his crisp dark hair to the soles of his well-shod feet. From where she stood, handing out refreshments, Sheena could see that Dawn's companion did not give the impression that he was enamoured of her presence. He was too cool, too delicately toned not to play the role of adoring suiter. Could Dawn not see that? She had experienced the advances of men, young though she was. Yet she was behaving completely out of character.

Presently Sheena was aware of someone speaking his name. Two models, friends of Dawn, were standing nearby munching savoury vol-au-vents.

'There's Ross Carlyle. Isn't he smashing? I wouldn't mind spending a night with him,' one sighed.

'No, but he might,' answered the other. 'Our Ross is choosy. But then he has only to crook a finger to whomsoever he might want and they come running. One would have to keep a man like him on a leash.'

Moving on, Sheena found herself wishing that she could have kept Dawn on a leash until such time that she was due to leave for the States. Her gaze was drawn again to her sister and the man in question.

Unwillingly her violet eyes seemed glued to his face. She saw those mobile lips move into words.

'See you later,' they formed in reply to something Dawn might have said about joining her other guests.

Dawn was gazing up at him like a schoolgirl on her first date and Sheena could have slapped her. Couldn't she see that he was filling in idle moments or did she really think he had come to the party specifically to see her? His male attraction was powerful. She could feel it from where she stood as he grinned down at her sister to make a playful feint beneath her chin with a gentle fist.

Good heavens, she scolded herself for allowing the pull of his personality to reach out to her. Until now she had been prepared to let him play the game he was playing knowing that any affair he cultivated with Dawn would be of short duration. By this time tomorrow night, Dawn would be on her way to America. It was that 'See you later,' bit which disturbed Sheena.

She saw Dawn reach up on tip-toe to kiss his cheek. How clever the man was in not bending his head to meet her lips. He was giving her a head start, letting her do the running until she had gone too far to turn back. Surely he knew why Dawn was giving the party? What did he care so long as he had his way? Sheena had not even met the man and already she despised him. It would be far better if she did not meet him. To be polite but aloof would be the best course of action where he was concerned.

Even so he looked so arrogant, so sure of himself that Sheena was of the opinion that no one had ever managed to get the better of him. Why should he have things his way? The tray she was carrying was almost empty and when one of the guests bore down on her to take the last of her delectable savouries, she placed the empty tray down near to the door and looked again across the room where the hateful man was hovering.

He was talking to one of the camera-men belonging to Dawn's team. Suddenly he lifted his dark eyes beyond his companion and met Sheena's gaze head on. Casually he took in the pretty evening dress in Indian print and the aura of auburn hair framing her oval face. Sheena felt her face go hot beneath that sardonic look.

The gold loop ear-rings were her only adornment and she knew there was nothing unusual about her to keep his interest. The expression in her eyes was wide and without guile, but she had none of Dawn's voluptuousness. She was slender as a willow with firm high breasts and a trim narrow waist suggesting an aura of healthy inner energy. This man's opinion of her did not mean a thing. To her chagrin, however, Sheena found it impossible to drag her gaze away from that dark, intent one. It was he who broke the communication between them by turning once more to his companion and, released, Sheena was surprised to find herself trembling.

Automatically she looked at her wristwatch, noted the time and looked around for her sister who was talking to the two models who had been discussing Ross Carlyle earlier. Swiftly she went over to join them.

'Time for Frank's telephone call,' she whispered urgently, and followed Dawn from the room.

They were in Dawn's bedroom when Sheena said thoughtfully, 'You didn't say that your new heart throb was coming to the party this evening.'

Dawn sat down on the bed, her hand resting on the telephone. In Sheena's opinion she had never looked so alive, so glittering and Sheena was sure that it was not the thought of speaking to her intended that had brought on such effervescent spirits.

Dawn's smile was provocative. 'Jealous because I didn't introduce you to him?' she scoffed without malice. 'So you noticed him? I'm sure every other woman in the room did, too.'

Sheena said coldly, 'Is he that notorious?'

Dawn laughed, lifted the receiver of the telephone and dialled a number. She said, 'Hello. Is that the airport? . . . I wonder if I could alter my flight to the States for the day after tomorrow? The details are . . .'

'Dawn, you can't . . . not after everything has been arranged,' Sheena gasped in horror. 'You don't know what you are doing. If you cancel that flight you know you'll never go to the States to marry Frank. Are you sure that you know what you are doing? You are giving up a chance of happiness for a mess of pottage. This man Ross is a philanderer if ever I saw one.' She looked pleadingly at her sister. 'Please, Dawn, don't do anything rash. Does this man Ross know that this is a farewell party for you?'

'In a way.'

A little hopelessly, Sheena said, 'What do you mean, in a way? That means you haven't told him that you are going to Boston to be married. Oh . . . well if this is what you want, but for heaven's sake don't tell Frank that you've changed your mind about marrying him. You could live to regret it.'

Dawn had aborted her call and was silent as Sheena sat down on the arm of a chair. Then she said, 'I want a little more time, that's all. I've promised to dine with Ross tomorrow evening.'

Sheena rose to her feet. 'In that case I shall be leaving in the morning.'

'Don't be like that. The lease on the apartment has a little while to run. You could stay here until the lease is up. I might ask Frank to keep it on for when we come over from the States. You might even get a job in London,' she said in a rush. 'I just have to see Ross again before I leave, that's all.'

Sheena's determination wavered. There was no reason for her to rush off back home and if she stayed over it was possible that she could stop Dawn from doing anything foolish. For all she knew, her sister could be genuinely in love with the new man in her life and if she was, who was she to try and stop her? It would not be right.

'I'll think about it,' she answered as the telephone buzzed.

Dawn picked it up. 'It's Frank,' she said covering up the mouthpiece with her hand.

Sheena nodded and left the room. She was on her way to the rest of the guests in the main lounge after threading her way past groups talking and laughing in odd corners. Someone had put on a record player and others were dancing in one corner of the room. Suddenly she was confronted by Ross Carlyle. There was an unmistakable gleam in his dark eyes. Sheena found herself thinking idiotically that no man should have such dark, thick curling lashes.

He deliberately blocked her view of everyone else in the room giving her the feeling that they were in a world of their own—just the two of them isolated from the rest of mankind.

'I am looking for the hostess,' he explained. 'She appears to have disappeared.'

'Dawn is on the telephone making a long distance call,' Sheena said meaningly.

'Then we mustn't disturb her, must we?' he drawled in a deep, melodic voice. 'Will you tell her that I have to leave now, but that I will see her tomorrow evening as planned. The name is Ross Carlyle.'

Sheena hesitated, her mind on Dawn and the outcome of her telephone conversation with Frank. With a start she saw that his expression was both mocking and amused. Regaining her senses, Sheena felt her heart pounding in her breast. His nearness was making her oddly breathless. Whatever was the matter with her? She had met men before, had admirers and enjoyed dates with them, but not one had affected her in this alarming way.

To her disgust she began to stammer, her voice cracking with nervous tension. 'I'll . . . give Dawn . . . your . . . your meassage . . . er . . . Mr Carlyle,' she said huskily.

The dark eyes narrowed down at her. 'You look familiar. Have I seen you some place before?' he murmured.

The scorn in her violet eyes lashed him. 'Oh, come on, Mr Carlyle, surely you can do better than that?' she scoffed.

He raised a dark brow. 'I don't think that you and I are talking on the same wave length, Miss . . . Miss,' he drawled maddeningly. 'You know my name, but I don't know yours.'

Sheena lifted her chin. 'There is no reason why you should know it,' she told him coolly.

'Why? Is it a secret?'

'No. But it can't be of any interest to you.'

'How do you know?'

'Because we aren't likely to meet again.'

His regard was shrewd and he said bitingly, 'When I asked just now if we had met before I was not making a pass at you. You resemble someone I know.' His eyes raked her face and deliberately roved slowly over her slender figure. He took his time in summing her up, taking in the wide violet eyes, the halo of auburn hair, the classically cut nose and enchanting mouth. Then his eyes moved downwards to the pulse beating in the hollow of her slender neck, the creamy skin showing a tantalizing glimpse of her firm young breasts where they rose beneath the neckline of her dress. By the time his gaze had reached her narrow waist and moved down to the dainty high-heeled sandals on her feet Sheena felt like hitting him.

'Yes, the likeness is there, but hardly discernible,' he murmured almost to himself. 'There is a similarity around the eyes perhaps, but there is more fire in your colouring . . . more passion. Your sister is only a paler version, shall I say?'

Sheena had felt her hackles rising for some time, but was further incensed when he took hold of her chin and lifted up her face. It was bad enough for him to snub her over mistaking his motives. It was quite another thing when he took hold of her face. How dared he?

'When you've quite finished, Mr Carlyle . . .' she began angrily.

Unperturbed he moved his thumb gently along her jaw line.

'It's Sheena is it not? Sheena Denton, sister of Dawn. Nice to meet you.'

His dark head moved nearer and she held her breath thinking for one dread moment that he was going to kiss her, but he drew back and she was amazed at her disappointment because he had not. His hand fell away and she felt curiously bereft of his touch. It was clear to her that he was no fool. He had seen the likeness between her and Dawn which was barely obvious except to the most perceptive of people.

Lips that would have softened to his kiss barely moved in a cool little smile. 'Mr Carlyle.' He acknowledged her address with a slow nod. 'I will give my sister your message. Shall I show you to the door?'

He gave another brief movement of the head, but Sheena was startled by the gleam in his eyes. 'Good night, Sheena. I will show myself out.'

She had an urge to wipe the heat from her brow. The spot where those long sensitive fingers had rested still tingled from his touch. What a man. No wonder Dawn was bowled over by him. She could understand her being knocked out for six. Poor girl—what chance had Frank against such charm and arrogance. Sheena returned to her sister's room after seeing that the two women helpers who were taking care of refreshments were coping with the demands of the guests. Her meeting, or was it a collision, with Ross Carlyle had been painfully enlightening. That gleam in his eyes as he had taken his leave was disturbing. He would make an implacable enemy. On the other hand she trembled to think what kind of a lover he would make. The colour burned her face on recalling her own part in the affair. She was not proud of it. Her behaviour had been that of a hard-bitten school ma'am, but it had been his fault entirely.

Whatever Dawn decided, Sheena would find it impossible to stay any longer in London.

CHAPTER TWO

SHEENA bumped into her sister at the door of her room.

'I have a message from your new boyfriend to say that he has to go and that he will see you tomorrow evening as arranged,' she said without preamble. 'How did the telephone conversation go or shouldn't I ask?'

Dawn leaned against the door-frame looking resigned. 'I have decided to go to the States after all,' she said. 'I'm even a little relieved that Ross has gone.'

Sheena stared in bewilderment. 'You are?' She made a gesture of helplessness. 'I think we had better join the guests, don't you?'

Dawn nodded. 'We'll talk about things later.'

The party did not break up until the small hours. Both sisters slept in until well after lunch. Sheena was up first to make coffee, and took a cup to Dawn.

'Everything is ready for you to go,' she said placing the tray in front of her sister as she sleepily pushed herself up in bed. 'I've decided to go home tomorrow after all. I can see no point in staying. Even if I managed to get a job here in London I couldn't afford the accommodation prices they are asking, and I don't intend staying here. It wouldn't be right.'

Dawn sipped her coffee. 'Why not? Frank is going to keep the flat on, so if you stay it will be as good as having a caretaker. There is nothing for you if you go back home. Why not sell the place?' She grinned at her sister's surprised expression. 'Don't look so shocked. Frank and I had a long talk and he thinks that by keeping on this apartment he will give me a sense of security while I am in the States. I shall still have one foot in the UK, so to speak. Besides he is worried about you being out of a job. It was different before we decided to get married. There were the two of us, you and me. I could have helped out.'

Sheena felt a jolt in her solar plexus as she wondered how much Frank knew of her own personal sacrifices during Dawn's illness and remembered just how much her sister had helped out after her salary as a top model had soared. She hadn't helped a bit. Sheena smiled palely. 'I take it that you didn't tell Frank about your illness?'

'Of course not.' Dawn looked peevish as she poured out more coffee. 'I'm not likely to am I? Can't have him thinking that he might have a sickly wife on his hands. Not that he will think that, though. I'm fully recovered and very fit. I couldn't stand the pace of my job if I wasn't.'

'I know you are and I agree with you, only you will be sure to tell your new doctor if you ever get pregnant, won't you? It's most important that he should know. I'd feel happier if you promised me that you would.'

Dawn said emphatically, 'As I don't intend to start a family, the necessity won't ever arise, so let's forget it shall we? What about Ross?'

'What about Ross?' Sheena sank down on to the bed. The merest mention of him gave her a horrid premonition.

'I'm supposed to dine with him this evening.'

'Then telephone the man and tell him that it's all off.'

'I can't. I don't know where to get in touch with him. When he takes off like he did last night, no one knows where he can be reached.'

'Can't you at least try to get in touch with him? What about his office? Can't you leave a message?'

'He won't be going to his office. He told me last night that he was waiting for an important telephone call which could take him away from the party. Poor Ross he will be so disappointed when he has to dine alone.'

'Poor Ross?' Sheena echoed explosively. 'Why he won't be a bit put out if you don't turn up. It might just do him good, for once, to be let down on a date. You do like him, don't you?'

Dawn looked uncomfortable. 'Of course I do. That's why I don't want to see him again in case I change my mind about going to the States,' she confessed sheepishly. 'After talking to Frank last night I realise that he is the best thing to have happened to me. Being a successful model is very demanding and these days one has to take a lot of stick from other women who are just waiting to get into your shoes . . . and there's the added problem of all the predatory males who like to lurk around every corner in the business. No, I am getting out.'

Sheena said quietly, 'There is nothing to prevent you from dining with this Ross person if you want to . . . providing that you know what you are doing.'

Dawn sighed. 'I didn't tell you, but Frank has friends flying back to the States on the same plane as I am, early tomorrow morning and they have invited me to have dinner with them this evening. They are a Mr and Mrs Oppenheimer. They are calling for me about seven o'clock to take me to this delightful little place they know on the Thames.'

Everything had been completed, bags packed, air tickets and other essentials checked and Dawn was ready waiting for Frank's friends to arrive. Restlessly she paced the apartment, frequently going to peer through the windows in expectation of their arrival. She looked round as Sheena put the last of her sister's baggage in the hall.

Petulantly, she said, 'I wish you would stop making

yourself useful and come to talk to me. I hate this hanging around—I think I'll have another drink.'

'For goodness' sake sit down,' Sheena said. 'You don't want to be blind drunk when these people arrive. I've got everything ready for your departure tomorrow, just in case you are late coming in tonight. There won't be much time in the morning.'

Dawn perched on the arm of a chair and looked cross. 'I wish you would decide to stay on here for a time. It won't cost you anything. You could go out to dinner with Ross in my place this evening, and explain to him why I had to rush off.'

Sheena looked her straight in the eye. 'Supposing I did go in your place, what explanation should I give?'

'Ross doesn't know about Frank and he didn't stay long enough last evening to hear the speeches and see the presentations from my colleagues. I intended to tell him, but I found I couldn't. You see Ross and I had the kind of rapport ... I don't think you would understand.'

'Try me,' Sheena said drily. 'If by "rapport" you mean sex appeal, then I do understand, because your Ross had the same effect on me.'

Dawn's thickly lashed grey eyes shot open. 'Is that why you are so anxious to be rid of me?'

'What do you mean, Dawn? I am merely pointing out to you that what you feel for Ross Carlyle is just the sort of healthy physical attraction a man or woman has for the opposite sex,' Sheena said earnestly. 'I haven't got a crush on your boyfriend, in fact he is the kind of man I would instinctively sheer away from. He's too much of a womaniser for my liking.'

Dawn shrugged bare shoulders. She was wearing a strapless dress in oyster silk that clung lovingly to her slim figure and featured a slit down one side-seam that, as she walked, showed the enchanting curve of her long legs. A black silk evening cape lined with the same oyster silk lay over the back of a chair, on top of that lay her evening-bag.

'I suppose he is more than you would be able to handle at that,' she said, not unkindly. 'After all I have had lots of experience with the male of our species. But, seeing that you aren't impressed by him, why won't you take my place this evening and deliver a little note for him, from me? Your obvious dislike of him will ensure that he stays at arm's length.'

'Because I am not the one he invited. His disappointment would be twofold. First, that you did not show up. Second, that it was me who did. Besides I don't think he would take lightly to being deceived.'

Dawn's silver grey eyes mirrored her calculating thoughts.

'Very well,' she acceded reluctantly. 'I do insist though that you give me your word not to tell Ross about Frank—that is, if you do meet him.'

'As I don't expect to see Ross again, the possibility of my doing so does not arise. If it makes you feel any better, though, I give you my word that I won't ever mention Frank to Ross.'

The buzz of the doorbell alerted them both and Dawn, pausing long enough to smooth her dress over the provocative curve of her hips, then glided to the door. Swiftly Sheena left the room, knowing that her sister would not want her to meet the Oppenheimers in case they asked if she was going to Boston for the wedding. They would certainly think it odd that she was not.

The Oppenheimers did not stay for a drink as they had to make a fairly long drive to the restaurant and they left with Dawn almost right away. When they had gone, Sheena had never felt so alone. She came back to the living-room aware of Dawn's five matched pieces of monogrammed luggage enveloped in the canvas travel covers, standing in the hall along with the small dressing-case she carried on her trips abroad. This time, though, Dawn would not be coming back for quite some time.

The heavy aroma of Dawn's favourite expensive French perfume lingered in the air of the room . . . Sheena sighed. She did hope that her sister was doing the right thing in not seeing Ross Carlyle again. After all the decision affected her whole future. Sheena did not believe in arranging people's lives and although Dawn was younger than herself by two years Sheena knew that her sister was far more experienced in life than she was herself. Aimlessly she wandered around the room, her arms tucked mandarin fashion into the loose sleeves of her wrap, feeling hopeless and helpless. The whole evening lay before her like a woefully empty stretch of time without purpose.

Wandering to her sister's bedroom to tidy it up, she paused by the pile of clothes Dawn had thrown out earlier and which she herself had folded neatly on to a chair. There was a letter on the top and a note. The letter had Ross Carlyle's name written on it. The note was to Sheena and read, 'Do what you like with the clothes. If Ross calls perhaps you will give him the letter. I still think you are a fool for not delivering it to him personally. I did not cancel the taxi which Ross has hired to collect me in the hope that you will change your mind and go.'

Sheena stared at the lavender coloured, perfumed envelope for a long time. Here was her chance to find out if Ross really did care for her sister. It would set her mind at rest that Dawn was doing the right thing in going to the States to marry Frank. Instant rapport did happen between people, even for the unromatic kind like Dawn. Sheena looked at her watch. There was still time to get ready. Her first reaction to her decision to go was one of relief, but as she dressed and applied her make-up Sheena began to feel decidedly nervous.

A centre parting to her luxurious auburn hair sent it cascading down in natural waves and curls to her slender shoulders. There was no problem about her choice of dress. On her limited income Sheena believed in buying clothes that were easy to wear, of good cut and design and simple to care for. With separates one could not go wrong. Her choice was a soft, pretty front wrap skirt with softly pleated gathering at the trim waist, a sleek little sleeveless scoop-necked top and an elegantly simple cardigan style jacket. The neckline of the top had pretty rimaldi edging in self-fabric of a cornflour blue that echoed the violet of her eyes.

Sheena was glad that the cut of her outfit emphasised her soft curves to give her an air of sophistication. She had no doubt that the women Ross Carlyle normally wined and dined would have heaps of glamour and *savoir-vivre* so it was important that she had to look like the kind of woman he would have asked out for the evening. When the taxi cab came she walked out to it with as much sang-froid as she could muster, but her steps faltered when once she found herself in the hotel foyer.

It helped to know that she was a stranger to the people in evening dress in the stream of diners entering the restaurant. Like the lighting the sound of clinking silverware and glasses was subdued in an atmosphere of luxury and good taste.

'Madame has a table?' said a discreetly quiet voice at her elbow and she turned with a start to find a waiter at her side.

'I . . . I think so,' she stammered. 'Sheena . . . I mean Dawn Denton.'

'Ah, yes. Mr Carlyle's guest. This way, Madame.'

She was led to a table behind an arrangement of cascading ferns and was politely helped into her seat. Almost at once the wine waiter was there uncorking a bottle and with a flourish poured out a little white wine for her to taste. Sheena sampled it and discovered that she could become quite partial to a medium dry vintage. She nodded her approval and he filled her glass. Raising her glass to the absent Ross, she was not sure whether she would have preferred him to be there or not.

The tables around her were rapidly filling up and it was not going to be fun eating alone. A waiter brought the menu and she studied it. The wine gave her Dutch courage and she wondered impishly whether she was only allowed to order certain things. Everything on the menu was deliciously expensive and she teetered between the lobster and . . .

'This way, Mr Carlyle. The lady has already arrived.'

The waiter's smooth, polite tones smote through her reverie like a blade and Sheena lifted wide violet eyes from the menu to see Ross Carlyle taking the seat opposite to her at the table. Automatically she steeled herself for his angry reaction to the absence of Dawn, but he did not bat an eyelid. Sheena, however, was not so cool. The explanation along with Dawn's letter which she had intended producing from her evening-bag was not forthcoming.

She was beyond words. In desperation she gulped down the wine and choked on it. Tears streamed down her face as she coughed, and a handkerchief was thrust across the table and she took it nervously.

'Sorry I am late,' he murmured. 'Is the wine not to your taste, my love?'

He beckoned to a waiter as Sheena mopped her eyes and attempted to regain her composure. He had brought in the tang of fresh air. It was there in his ruddy tan, in the clearness of his liquid dark eyes and the sudden flash of his teeth as he had spoken to her. But that smile had not reached his eyes.

She wondered if he had called to collect Dawn at the apartment for he had certainly had time to wash and and change into the impeccable evening suit which fitted his wide shoulders with a military smartness. Sheena had to admit that he looked immaculate and rather dangerous, a man whose appearance put an extra percentage on the bill.

She discreetly returned the large white handkerchief, which he received politely and returned to his pocket. Then he placed clasped hands on the table to look right into her eyes.

'A funny thing happened to me this evening,' he began and broke off as the waiter returned with a bottle of wine.

The wine was approved and two glasses were filled. Ross lifted his glass. There was a wicked gleam in his eyes.

'Cheers,' he said coolly. 'Where was I? Ah, yes. A very funny thing happened to me this evening. I had this date with a platinum blonde and she turned out to be a redhead. Now how could such a thing have happened?'

Sheena felt her heart pounding madly and she was breaking out into a cold sweat. Well, if he was not going to behave like a gentleman she would play him at his own game.

'Perhaps the lady had an auburn rinse,' she replied. 'It has been known to happen.'

'You are not going to suggest that she also might be wearing contact lenses to change her eyes from grey to the colour of drenched violets?' he mocked.

Sheena aware of her still moist lashes blinked hard and tried to look at ease. 'Stranger things have happened,' she said. 'Did you have a good day?' She was surprised at her own coolness as Ross choked slightly on his drink.

'Usual run of the mill,' he murmured. 'But I hope to brighten it up a little this evening. Life is full of surprises and unexpected situations. Don't you think so, Sheena?'

He picked up the menu she had put down and studied it as he waited for her answer.

'I . . . I suppose . . . it is,' she stammered. 'I haven't thought much about it. I am sorry you have been so disappointed this evening, I . . .'

She looked up at the waiter who had appeared to take their order then moved her gaze to the impassive face of her companion.

Ross raised a dark brow. 'Is there anything special you prefer, my love, or shall I order for us both?'

Sheena had a wild desire to giggle hysterically. It was all so funny, Ross treating her as his lady friend when she knew that it would have given him the greatest pleasure to strangle her.

'I'm easy,' she replied. 'You order.'

When the waiter had gone, Ross said, 'That is a relief.'

'I don't quite follow . . .' she said with a worried little frown on her smooth forehead.

'The fact that you are easy. The evening will have its compensations after all.' There was a gleam in his eyes and it was evident that he was not amused.

'I still don't understand what you mean,' she said uneasily.

'You will.' His relaxed tone of voice and that gleam she was beginning to read in his dark eyes were sending her into a kind of panic. He seemed predatory and challenging.

'I think the time has come for me to . . .' she began firmly when the waiter appeared with their first course.

Ross said blandly, 'I trust you like smoked salmon. You were saying . . .'

'Oh, yes. I . . .'

Again he interrupted her this time lifting a long brown hand. 'I must apologise. I never enquired as to whether you were a vegetarian or not.' His white smile was mocking. 'Or even if you were on a diet.' He slowly looked her over and insolently scrutinised the pretty outfit, his eyes lingering on her small firm, pointed breasts. 'You look as slim and tender as a young willow which could mean that you bend easily.'

Sheena swallowed nervously. It was just as she had thought—the man was positively dangerous, but surely he could do her no harm in a public dining-room full of people. She was appalled at the arrogance of him in thinking that she had gatecrashed in order to see him again. Anger gave her a coolness and dignity which sat well on her slender shoulders.

'I don't think that you should underestimate the willow,' she advised him sweetly. 'It is sometimes very, very tough to handle.'

Sheena came to a decision while speaking. There was no way she would allow him to pay for her meal. She would insist upon paying for her own, no matter what he said, and the sooner it was over the better. When the time came, she would ask for her own bill and leave him with Dawn's letter. Feeling better at having devised a plan of action she began to eat her portion of delicious smoked salmon. As she tilted her gaze down to her plate, though, she saw that predatory gleam change to one of admiration. Goodness! she thought. I am provoking his interest in me—just the thing I want to avoid. It would perhaps be better to appear more amenable.

'You could be right, but a man has ways of tackling stubborn things.' Ross's answer came after a few moments of obvious consideration.

'And stubborn people?' she queried, with innocent wide violet eyes looking unflinchingly into his dark ones. 'By the way, I am sorry that Dawn could not come this evening. I have a letter of explanation for you in my bag.'

He gestured with a lazy hand. 'Leave it until later. I'd much rather hear you tell me about yourself.'

'There's nothing to tell. Dawn is the one who has an interesting life. Mine is very dull.'

He raised a dark brow. 'You surprise me. Do you work here in London?'

'No.'

'You don't work?'

He leaned forward to refill her wine glass. His long brown fingers curling round the bottle were lean and strong with neatly manicured nails. He had a signet ring on the third finger of his right hand.

'Not at the moment.'

'You are not very forthcoming, are you?' he said drily.

'Why are you so interested?' she queried. 'I'm not in the least bit curious about you.' Sheena felt the hot colour flood beneath her clear skin as she realised that, in fact, this was not true. She would love to know all about him. He was the first man she had met who was . . . different from the others. To her amazement she wanted the evening to go on and never end.

The waiter brought more delicious food and when he had gone Sheena said, 'I think that anything you have to say will be more intriguing than my life-story. You must have had plenty of interesting experiences.'

He looked at her intently for several seconds then he went on to ask her what she had seen of London. She told him and he looked interested when she admitted to being on holiday.

'Are you staying until Dawn gets back?' he asked.

'Gets back?' Sheena echoed foolishly, then she

realised that he did not know about her sister and Frank. 'Oh, no. I am going back home.'

'Where is home?'

'The Midlands.'

'You are being evasive again,' he said.

'And you are being more than curious.'

He smiled. 'What would you like to do when we leave here?'

'Why, go back to my sister's apartment, of course,' she replied a little breathlessly.

He raised a dark brow. 'Isn't the night a trifle young to completely abandon it at such an early hour? After all, you did say that you are on holiday?'

'I was on holiday,' she corrected him, 'but I go back home tomorrow.'

'Is it necessary for you to go back tomorrow?' His dark eyes narrowed a little as he gazed at her intently.

'Yes. I have to find myself a job. I haven't got one at the moment, you see.'

'Why not seek a job here in London? What are your qualifications?'

Sheena bridled. 'You sound like a clerk at the unemployment agency. What has it to do with you?'

'I'm interested.'

'Because I am Dawn's sister?'

'If you like.'

Sheena bridled still more. 'I'm sorry, but it has nothing to do with you.'

'We seem to knock sparks off one another. I wonder why?' he murmured and leaned over once again to fill up her wine glass.

Sheena realised then that she had been sipping her wine more often than she had intended, in order to avoid his steadfast gaze. It made a change from looking down on her plate as she ate.

Hastily she covered the top of her wine glass with a

slender hand. 'No more for me, thanks. I'm not a great wine drinker,' she confessed.

His smile was mocking. 'Playing safe?' He frowned. 'I'm puzzled as to why you came here this evening. Why didn't you leave the letter with one of the staff here? They would have seen that I received it.'

She avoided his gaze. 'I was curious about you,' she admitted in a low voice.

'In what way?' Ross sat back in his chair and his long, brown fingers toyed with the stem of his wine glass.

'Not in the way you think . . .' she began. Searching for the right words, Sheena was relieved to see the waiter arriving with their coffee. It was awfully difficult to explain and Ross seemed determined not to help her out.

'So, you were curious. Do go on,' he urged when the waiter had gone. Again he leaned back in his chair, giving her his full attention. It was something in his favour that he did not look around, but concentrated upon her.

'Your intentions regarding Dawn,' she began warily, knowing that she had to be careful not to give her sister away.

He grimaced. 'You mean, are my intentions towards her honourable?' He threw back his head and laughed, a deep chuckle of mirth that filled her with fury. 'I've met your sister about half a dozen times in all. What do you expect—that I should propose marriage?'

Her throat went dry. 'What did you say? I understood that she had only met you the other evening and that you left a profound impression upon her.'

'Really! And you want to know what kind of an impression she had left on me. Am I right?'

'Yes.' Sheena picked up her coffee cup to find that her hand was trembling.

She wondered if he really was aware of his physical attraction for the opposite sex, and Dawn had lied to her about their meetings. Something indefinable crept into his eyes as he stared at her and for an uneasy moment Sheena thought it was time she went back to her apartment . . . She gritted her teeth. Why should she be intimidated by this arrogant man and warned off before she discovered the truth?

With a hollow feeling in her stomach, she recalled long exhausting hours she had passed in nursing her sister back to health, willing her to recover. The surgeon had warned her that Dawn would always have to be careful and not overdo things. Youthful resilience would help a lot, but there was still the need to take care. She had made light of it to Dawn, not wanting to worry her, but her sister had discovered her own limitations and Sheena had been so relieved to hear that she was marrying someone who would look after her.

If only this man sitting opposite to her had not turned up in her sister's life, then she would not be here herself asking the impossible of him. What man would honestly admit his intentions towards a very pretty girl? Certainly not Ross Carlyle who could have most any girl by merely crooking a long, brown finger.

She sipped at her coffee and broke the silence, wishing that he did not look at her so intently. 'No doubt you think it is cheek on my part,' she said with difficulty. 'Especially after telling you what I do is none of your business. The thing is, that I care a lot for my sister and I was worried.'

Ross had drunk his coffee and reached for the coffee pot in order to refill his cup. She shook her head as he held the spout over her cup.

'You were worried that I was going to seduce her?'

It was her turn to laugh. 'Oh, no. Dawn is not so naïve that she could be easily seduced.'

She watched him put down the coffee pot and she found a strange delight in looking at his long brown hands. They were strong and looked as if they could be both gentle and ruthless, she thought, then looked up to find his eyes once more upon her.

'Then why are you worried?' he demanded.

Sheena finished her coffee and put down her cup. 'Because I think that you bowled her over. Dawn reacted to you as she has never reacted to any man—at least any man I know of.'

'So?'

'I wondered,' she replied, her deep blue eyes wide with apprehension as they met his. 'I wondered if you felt the same way about her?'

He laughed as though her question was absurd. His eyes mocked. 'And if I do?'

She bit her lip to prevent it trembling. 'If you do then I have done her a great wrong in persuading her to go to the States,' she confessed unhappily.

'But surely you had nothing to do with Dawn going? This was just another modelling assignment, was it not?'

Sheena went cold inside, remembering her promise not to mention Dawn's relationship with Frank to this man. However the promise had been overruled by the need to tell the truth. She nodded and thought of Dawn's letter in her purse.

'It is just possible, however, that Dawn will marry while she is in the States.'

'And you think that could be wrong if your sister and I are interested in each other?' he mocked. 'You think that we could be soul mates?'

She said furiously, 'There is no need to be sarcastic about it. I don't want her to ruin her life by marrying the wrong man. Don't you see?'

Coolly, he said, 'No. I don't.'

Desperately, Sheena hissed, 'She wanted to stay and see you again and I persuaded her to go. I don't interfere as a rule, but I thought this feeling she had for you was only a phase she was going through because of her uncertainty about this ardent admirer in Boston.'

'And it would make you feel happier about persuading her to leave, to know that I have no serious intentions for your sister . . . that our eyes did not meet across a crowded room and all that romantic nonsense?'

Sheena began to laugh and she laughed until tears stung her eyes. It was quiet laughter, deep and infectious.

He frowned. 'What's the joke?'

She sobered and wiped tears from her lashes with a finger.

'Our eyes met across a crowded room, yours and mine at Dawn's party. I just remembered,' she gulped.

'Want to make something of it?' he challenged.

'Good heavens, no,' she replied swiftly. Opening her evening purse she drew out Dawn's letter to him.

He waved it to one side. 'Later,' laconically.

'But when?' She reached out and placed the letter in front of him. 'I think you had better pick it up and read it, because I can see another argument looming. I want to pay for my meal myself, if you don't mind.'

His eyes narrowed. He was not amused. 'The bill has already been settled.'

He rose to his feet and came round to pull out her chair. As she rose to her feet and stood by him she was aware of his height and the width of his shoulders. He had tucked Dawn's letter into the inside pocket of his jacket—over his heart, she thought idiotically and walked out of the hotel with him. He held himself with a masculine grace, walking with the nonchalant ease of active and supple muscles. He was too dynamic, too virile for Dawn's cold nature unless . . . Sheena was amazed at her own deductions. She was allowing herself to be carried away by the man's splendid physique, his wide shoulders, narrow hips and long legs.

At the hotel entrance, he paused and looked down at her.

'Where would you like to go now?' he enquired politely.

'Back to my apartment.'

He sighed and his eyes roved over her in the manner of someone who looks, and absorbs every detail of his subject within seconds. Sheena quivered inwardly. If ever there was a prime example of the predatory look, this is it, she thought, as his eyes rested on her prettily shaped mouth before moving down to the creamy skin revealed by the scooped neckline of her top.

'It's all right, I'll take a taxi,' she said firmly in an effort to bring his attention back from the critical appraisal of her trim waist and firm, softly rounded breasts.

'The pleasure is mine, Sheena.' He smiled very dangerously and lifted a hand to hail an approaching cab. 'We can go to my apartment.'

'What for?' Sheena breathed tightly, wondering what she had let herself in for. Maybe he had other ideas as to how she could pay for her meal.

'It's private enough for our talk,' he said, helping her into the cab.

'What talk?' she asked as he dropped into the space beside her.

'You want to know how I feel about your sister. I shall read her letter and let you know,' he said as calmly as if she had made some enquiry about the weather or the shares index.

CHAPTER THREE

'BUT you can't base your feelings for Dawn on what you read in her letter,' she protested when later they were seated in a luxurious apartment decorated in shades of beige and brown, carpeted with thick white Wilton and tastefully appointed to produce an air of sybaritic elegance.

'I wasn't aiming to,' he answered giving her the coffee she had requested. She had been careful to sit on a chair instead of one of the long sofas, thus ensuring that he could not sit beside her. He had made the coffee in a matter of moments and while he busied himself at the task, Sheena looked around the dimly lit room and tried to calm her tattered nerves. She dared not explore too extensively, but would have liked to have been able to comment on the decor of that portion of the room she could immediately see. She would have liked to make some impersonal conversation about the subtle mixture of muted colours that came to life when he switched the wall-lights on. The apartment seemed very large and in spite of herself Sheena became aware of her desire to see the rest of it, but she dared not move from where he had left her and felt disinclined to ask him to show her around.

Ross emerged from the kitchen and she watched him sit down opposite her in a chair that matched her own. As he took out Dawn's letter from his pocket, he gestured to the dish of cashew nuts and almond fancies that he had placed on the low table to the side of her chair.

'Help yourself,' he said. 'Please excuse me for a

moment while I read this.' He lowered his eyes to the letter.

'From what I can see, this is not quite what I would have expected of a bachelor flat in London. It seems very opulent and looks to be rather larger than I might have thought.'

'Hmm? I'm sorry . . . Oh, yes, the apartment. Would you like to take a look around?'

'No, thanks.'

'It's quite different to your sister's place . . . and you won't get another chance to see it if you go home tomorrow. Why don't you stay in London for a while? Dawn tells me the lease on her flat has almost a year to run.' He frowned as if something bothered him. 'It must cost a bomb to rent.'

Sheena nodded. 'It does, but Dawn shared the rent with two other models until they got married.'

She wanted to tell him that she had come for a holiday the day after Dawn's two flatmates moved out, but she could not. Neither could she tell him that Frank had taken over the lease. She wondered what was in the letter to make Ross as thoughtful as he had been since he had started reading it, and she moved uneasily.

'Have you decided to tell me what your true feelings are for Dawn? I would like to know honestly so that I can feel I did the right thing in persuading her not to see you again. I might add that it wasn't only my persuasion that finally convinced her. I do, however, feel very much to blame for her going.'

Ross reached for an ivory cigarette box from the low table beside him and flicked it open. 'Cigarette?' he said.

She shook her head. 'I don't smoke. In any case I could not aff . . .' Sheena broke off wishing she had guarded her tongue more.

A dark eyebrow raised mockingly made her blush for

some reason. 'You were going to say that you could not afford it. Why don't you get a job?' He had helped himself to a cigarette and held it up in a gesture of asking her permission. Sheena nodded in a daze.

'I beg your pardon,' she said stiffly.

He used a monogrammed cigarette lighter which he replaced in his pocket and inhaled before blowing out a thin line of smoke away from her.

'I said, why don't you get a job?'

'That's what I thought you said. I am still on holiday. A while ago you were suggesting I stayed on here for longer.'

'You could do both,' he suggested.

'I'll think about it,' she replied realising that his expression was rock hard. Hastily she drank her coffee. He was getting personal again and so it was time for her to go. Sheena rose to her feet and the next moment he was there beside her.

'You can't go yet. I haven't told you what you want to know about Dawn,' he argued, and crushed the cigarette in an ashtray.

Her breath went tight as his hands gripped her shoulders.

'I don't want to, anymore,' she replied desperately. 'I have to go now.'

'Why?' His lips curled in amusement and there were mocking glints in his eyes. 'You have been very brave to challenge a man about his lovelife and even beard him in his den, when you don't even like him. I wonder why?'

He was drawing her gradually towards him and she felt herself stiffening in his grasp. The faint aroma of his aftershave teased her nostrils and she pushed her hands against his wide unyielding chest. But it was too late. He had clamped her against him and she was tinglingly aware of the whole length of his virile figure crushed against her soft, yielding curves.

His dark head bent and his mouth rested upon her quivering lips in a determined but gentle kiss. She tried to move her head, but only once, for the magic of his lips was arousing sensations that she had never known before. Her heart was thundering into his chest and her head swam dizzily in confusion. With an expertise she might have guessed he would possess his mouth moved over hers, seductively sliding down to the pulsing hollow of her throat as his hands moved over her back leaving imprints that tingled with warmth.

Time slid magically by each second counting the duration of his passionate embrace, until Ross sensing her surrender again found her lips open to the gentle invasion of his tongue. It was then that Sheena came to her senses and she struggled frantically. He released her slowly, his jawline hardening as he looked down at her furious, bright, violet eyes and quivering lips.

'I ought to have known what to expect from you,' she cried scathingly. 'Men like you are all the same—out for what you can get. Goodbye, Mr Carlyle. I'm glad now that I helped to send Dawn away from you.'

She marched to the door her head held high in anger, but he was quicker. He moved to block her way and the anger in him seemed almost tangible.

'Are you really?' he said, his voice cold with fury. 'Is that the real reason you came to see me—out of concern for your sister? Tell me what kind of man do you think I am. Give me your honest opinion. What was your first impression of me?'

He folded his arms across his chest and waited for her to speak.

Sheena simmered down. She knew that she would come away from this meeting a sadder and wiser person for her foolhardy rush into contact with a man she knew to be a philanderer. She looked down at her hands that trembled around her evening-purse.

'I was very impressed,' she began honestly. 'I thought that you possessed a combination of good looks, virility and charm second to none and I could visualise all the women swooning at your feet. In fact I didn't blame Dawn one bit for being bowled over by you.'

He arched a dark brow. 'No?'

'No. I also thought that you were too good to be true. Your suave approach and that wicked self-confident gleam in your eyes convinced me that you were the very antithesis of a man who would make good husband material.'

'But you wanted to confirm your suspicions, and so you came to have dinner with me. Why did you come when you knew what kind of man I was or, at least, thought you did? Surely I didn't have to put in words what I felt about Dawn? It would have been irrelevant because you don't think me capable of any decent feelings at all.'

'I didn't say that.' Sheena lifted stormy eyes to meet his cool appraisal. 'I haven't finished yet. I think you are arrogant, and ruthless when you choose to be and I am sorry now that I came.'

'If you thought that I was arrogant and ruthless surely you knew that I was capable of running my own affairs—particularly those of a romantic or sexual nature. You knew damned well that if I had wanted your sister I would have taken her. Oh, no, that isn't the reason why you came this evening—it was just an excuse. You came for a free night out. Your tame meal ticket has taken flight to the States, so you are out for what you can get in the way of free hand-outs from her friends and acquaintances.'

Sheena was so appalled at this accusation that she just stared at him in gasping amazement. 'I beg your pardon,' she croaked on breath regained. 'Would you care to repeat that?'

'You heard the first time. Why don't you get a job and earn your little outings instead of being such a parasite on a sister who's younger and more hard-working than you are?'

The contempt in his eyes lashed her like a whip and she did the only thing possible under the circumstances. Her hand flew up and cracked, open-palmed, against his face. It was like the report of a pistol and she, herself, flinched at the impact. But Ross did not. There was an angry reddening imprint on his left cheek and she looked at it in horror. His mouth took on a cruel slant and he pulled her to him.

'So we are playing rough, are we?' he muttered and there was certainly nothing gentle about the way he grabbed her hair to keep her face upturned beneath his. It was too painful for her to struggle so Sheena had to endure his touch as he plundered her mouth in all its sweetness once more. Again the magic of his embrace played havoc with her emotions, and she was terrified of antagonising him further.

'I'm surprised that a hard little bitch like you has any softness in her nature,' he snarled when at last he lifted his head to look at her wide violet eyes and quivering mouth that was bruised by his kisses.

Sheena was confused. He must be talking about someone else. He could not possibly mean her. His hold on her had slackened, but his face did not soften its expression. In truth she cared very much what he thought about her and she had shown her desire for his regard by responding to his kiss in such an abandoned way. The thought of having to hold out against him, filled her with panic. She had to get away.

In one fluent movement she had pushed him away and made for the door. On the threshold she turned to see him sprawled in a chair.

'I was wrong to have seen you at all this evening,' she

admitted. 'Thanks for confirming what I thought about you in the first place. I was absolutely right.'

He slung a leg over the chair arm and did not attempt to rise out of the position she had pushed him into.

'To hear the truth about oneself is never palatable, is it?' he mocked. 'What I can't understand is why you should persuade Dawn to go away. You must dislike me an awful lot to send her away to your own disadvantage.'

Sheena frowned. 'Disadvantage?' she echoed.

'That's right. Your meal ticket has gone and you will have to get yourself a job, pay your own way. Unless you were hoping to hang on to me?'

'You keep referring to my meal ticket. Dawn has never kept me nor have I ever financially relied on her. In any case, I don't see what it has got to do with you.'

'At least I know that you had the holiday at her expense,' he said quietly.

'How dare you,' she blazed. 'You know nothing about it at all. Oh, and while we're on the subject—I nearly forgot.' She turned to face him, taking out two ten-pound notes from her purse. Going to the nearest low table, she laid the money on it. Then, with a look which she hoped would cut him down to size, she added icily, 'That's for my meal this evening. Goodbye, Mr Carlyle. If I ever see you again it will be too soon.'

Sheena did not breath freely until she reached the street. Thank goodness she had enough money to pay for a cab back to the apartment. On the way there she found that she was still quivering from the verbal lashing she had received from Ross Carlyle's tongue. Nothing he had said about her was true. Dawn and the two friends with whom she had shared the apartment, had done all the work between them in it. When Sheena had arrived, Dawn's two companions had already gone and it had been left to her to clean the apartment up.

She had also paid for all the food including Dawn's, and had done all the cooking, baking and housework.

Unlike her sister, Sheena was much too proud and independent to allow anyone else to keep her in any of the essentials. Her heart was still beating heavily in her breast as she entered the apartment, eased off her shoes, and flung herself into a chair. Leaning her head back she closed her eyes on a welter of emotions. Overriding them all was the humiliation of knowing Ross was of the opinion that she was a mere parasite, only out for what she could get. She was just not that kind of woman at all. How could she have put herself in that kind of situation anyway? Maybe he was right, maybe there had been an ulterior motive for her going out with him this evening. Was there perhaps some hidden force within her that had made her go out for one last fling before her holiday ended? Without realising it, had she yearned for one memorable evening to lighten the time ahead when she returned home to no job? Well, she had had her night out and she would have been better off without having it at all. There was no one to blame but herself.

At five o'clock the following morning Sheena had not slept a wink since the early hours when she had been awakened by the most violent pains in her stomach—indeed she had rushed to the bathroom to be sick. And so it had gone on through the night with each spasm of pain seeming worse than the last. Sheena was desperate with worry, trying to keep quiet and not wake Dawn who had to be up at a reasonable hour to catch her flight to Boston. By the time dawn cracked the dark sky in the east, she felt like a limp, wet, rag doll, falling back on to her tumbled sheets after yet another spell of wrenching nausea.

When Dawn had roused herself and prepared to make her journey to the airport she had been frantic with concern for Sheena and it was only by the use of a great deal of persuasion that Sheena had convinced Dawn that she would be perfectly all right on her own. After extracting from her sister a promise to call out a doctor if there was no improvement by lunchtime, Dawn had left with the Oppenheimers in a taxi to the airport.

Towards midday, Sheena began to feel incredibly thirsty, so she filled a jug with iced water and throughout the afternoon lay on her bed sipping the cool liquid and welcoming the fresh air that filtered through the open window. She would not be going home today that was for sure. Fortunately her coach and rail tickets were valid for a month so she could still use them if she stayed over for a few days.

Looking round the luxurious apartment with dull eyes Sheena found herself almost hating it now. It belonged to Dawn's world not to hers. Material possessions had never been very important to Sheena. She had seen so many of her friends, especially those that were married, consumed with an insatiable desire for all the luxuries of their better-off neighbours.

Though Sheena would have liked a nice home, there was no way she would have obtained it at the cost of more genuine possessions like the love of a husband and children. Sheena liked her freedom at the moment, so her thoughts had not dwelt on marriage. The two years she had given up everything in order to nurse Dawn, had taught her how valuable personal freedom was. Not that she resented nursing her sister through a critical period in her life. She would always be thankful that it had been her constant attention and care that had saved her sister's life.

Towards five o'clock that evening she had enjoyed an hour or two of fitful sleep, but was awakened by the insistent buzz of the doorbell. Surfacing from badly needed slumber it took Sheena some time before she was fully awake. Her mouth felt like sandpaper as she left her bed and drifted to the door. Who could it be? There were no tradesmen to call. Was it possible that Dawn had come back having changed her mind yet again? The caller was showing unusual impatience by keeping a constant pressure on the doorbell and her fingers were already on the door-catch when Sheena realised that she had no wrap over her flimsy nightdress. There had been no time to put on a wrap during her dashes to the bathroom to be sick and it had become a habit to leave her bed without reaching for it.

She almost groaned at the thought of how unpresentable she must look with no make up on her unwashed face, her hair all tousled and looking exactly how she felt—like death itself.

'Hello,' drawled Ross looking her over. 'How are you feeling after last evening?'

To say that Sheena was taken aback, was to put it mildly. With maddening slowness he glanced over her from the luxuriant auburn hair in disarray, to her bare feet. She doubted if he missed a scrap of her nakedness, mistily visible beneath the flimsy night dress. His eyes lingered on the pulse beating madly at the base of her throat, then on to the pointed tips of her firm young breasts before moving down to peruse her other delicious curves.

Sheena swayed under his scrutiny, then pulled herself together. 'This is hardly a sociable time to call.'

He consulted his wrist watch, his dark eyes slightly mocking. 'It is a little after five o'clock in the evening,' he murmured but his glance was keen. 'How are you feeling?'

'I was fine until you arrived,' she lied valiantly.

It was then that she saw his eyes looked tired, as if he too had been up half the night.

His hands were on her shoulders pushing her gently back to allow him to enter the apartment.

'Then all I can say is that if you are feeling fine, it's time you began to feel dreadfully ill,' he told her very determinedly. 'Your face is a pale shade of green and your eyes look enormous and heavy through lack of sleep. I'll wager that you have been up all night like me. Correct?'

Sheena found herself thinking that his height and breadth of shoulder put her at a disadvantage even when she had her high heeled shoes on, but in her bare feet he was much bigger and more menacing.

'So you have been sick as well?' she said, moistening dry lips as she backed slowly indoors. 'At least I know that you had no hand in it—you wouldn't have made yourself sick too.'

His hands had been about to release her shoulders, but now they gripped them mercilessly and he spoke, his voice taut with astonishment.

'Do you really think that I would inflict that kind of pain on another human being?' he demanded furiously. 'I wouldn't wish food-poisoning on my worst enemy. Get back in your bed before I forget that you are still sick.'

'If you think that I am going back to bed while you are here, you are sadly mistaken. Leave this apartment at once or I'll telephone for the police,' she threatened.

He shook her gently. 'And what would you charge me with? You let me in and you dined with me last evening.'

She felt the warmth of his hands through the delicate material of her nightdress as she tried to wriggle free. Suddenly she was swept up into his arms and he was striding with her into the bedroom through the open door. Putting her in bed he drew up and straightened the crumpled covering over her. Then he left the room.

In no time at all he was back with a tablespoon he had found in the kitchen and he was taking a bottle of thick white liquid from his pocket.

'Open your mouth,' he ordered after sitting her up in bed and plumping up the pillows behind her back. He tipped the white stuff down her throat and she swallowed. It was not unpleasant to taste and it felt very warming on the back of her throat. 'There, that wasn't too bad, was it?' he said, putting down the spoon on the bedside table and replacing the top of the bottle.

Sheena felt her stomach heave once as it went down. Then she closed her eyes, only vaguely aware of steadying fingers on the pulse at her wrist. A comforting warmth spread all over her body and she slept. When she awakened it was growing dusk.

'How are you feeling now?' Ross came into the room as if on cue. 'Ready for another dose of the medicine?'

Sheena stared at him in dismay. 'Haven't you gone yet? How long have I been asleep?'

'It's getting on for ten o'clock,' he answered. 'Has the pain gone?'

'Yes. I am all right now. It isn't necessary for you to stay,' she hastened to reassure him.

'I have to make sure that you are perfectly recovered. I really ought to send for the doctor . . .'

'Oh, no. I am perfectly all right now,' she insisted, closing her eyes to blot out his image.

He had taken off his jacket and he calmly sat down on to the edge of the bed. Then he lifted her up and rearranged the pillows behind her.

'I'm not an invalid,' she protested. 'Will you please go? I . . . I don't want your help now or at any time.' She glared at him. 'Only a cad would take advantage of a . . . person who was ill.'

'You just said that you were all right,' he reminded her. 'Let's try another dose of the medicine, shall we?'

His glance as it roved over her was searching. 'You are a better colour, but you look terribly washed out.'

Her face, pale in the shadowed light of the room, had an air of appealing distress. The daylight was being fast swallowed up in warm, perilous darkness and he was so near and somehow frightening.

She said faintly, 'If I promise to take the medicine will you leave?'

'I'll think about it,' was all he would say.

She felt his warmth as he held her steady with one hand at the back of her head while he tipped the spoonful of mixture down her throat. His closeness was unsettling, but she was glad of the medicine for it eased her tired stomach muscles and made her sleepy as he settled her down on her pillows.

She watched his long lean fingers straightening the bed clothes and wished that he would go.

'With a bit of luck you might sleep all night now,' he said as if he was hoping that she would.

'Why didn't you leave earlier?' she asked, sensing his coolness.

'Because I wanted to see if you were all right.'

'Well I am now. I'm grateful for what you have done for me. Thanks and good night.'

He raised a dark brow. 'Anyone would think that you couldn't stand the sight of me,' he quipped, looking down at her with a twisted smile.

'That's right. I can't.'

She noticed that the neck of his shirt was open showing his firm brown throat and hirsute chest. He looked strong and virile and very masculine. Why did he have to be so attractive? And why did there have to be an air of dependability about him that so readily encouraged a feeling of trust. But then she was not his kind of girl, was she? Had Dawn been in her place it might have been a different matter.

He said lazily, 'I bet you didn't like being sick either, but you have to bear these things. Actually it was lucky you were so sick, it could have saved your life.'

'I know,' she admitted dully.

He leaned down to gaze into her face and she flushed hotly as he placed the back of his fingers to her forehead, then her cheek.

'Are you hot?' he asked grimly.

'What can you expect when you bend over me like that. I feel embarrassed. I . . . I wish you would go.'

She was becoming more and more confused, and angry too. Of course she was hot and she went rosier when he sat down on the bed beside her. How could she tell him that his presence was unsettling and the clean scent of him as he leaned over to tuck a stray curl behind her ear was setting her heart thundering.

Softly, dangerously, he said, 'Surely you aren't embarrassed by a man in his shirt sleeves? I thought that breed of modest woman died out years ago.'

Sheena felt a shiver along her spine for he had brought that lean, good-looking face very near to her flushed one, and she inhaled the aromatic scent of good grooming. She was past speech as he gazed at the luminosity of her wide violet eyes and the parted lips that showed her small white teeth.

'So your eye lashes are real,' he marvelled, looking at the silkiness of their thick fringe. Suddenly those long, lean fingers were under her chin and she found herself floundering in the deep intensity of his gaze. Her senses reeled at his nearness as he filled her vision with his dark eyes, the breadth of his wide shoulders and the mocking curve of his lips. Then abruptly he let her chin go, and stood up.

'Good night,' she said pointedly now that he had removed himself from the bed, and closed her eyes.

When he had gone she felt depressed and disappointed. It had all been building up to an anti-climax and she felt as if she had been robbed of something. Sheena had fully expected him to kiss her. She would have given anything for tonight not to have happened. They had been the worst moments of her life. It was to be hoped that he had gone from the apartment because she had seen enough of Ross Carlyle for one day.

CHAPTER FOUR

It was a relief to Sheena to realise upon wakening the next morning that she had slept throughout the night. She did not feel too bad, just washed out and lethargic. Gingerly she swung her legs out of bed and stood up. Somehow she had not the energy to take a bath so she just washed her hands and face, combed her hair and cleaned her teeth. Her first impulse was to take a drink in the kitchen then go back to bed, but the thought that Ross might call again spurred her on to don cream trousers and a sleeveless primrose top.

Her reflection in the mirror was not too bad. Her eyes were clear enough and her face was fresh from her recent wash. It had never occurred to her that Ross would not go home the previous evening, so it was with surprise and dismay that she found him in a kitchen impregnated with the aroma of freshly made coffee.

'Oh! No!' she cried in dismay. 'Don't tell me that you have been here all night?' Taking a long breath she steadied herself. After all he was only making sure that she was all right. Nevertheless she stared unappeased at his fresh appearance in oatmeal trousers and white shirt which enhanced his dark good looks. 'I don't know why you stayed,' she added, amazed that he should be so at home in the kitchen.

Suddenly she was staring helplessly at the sausages, bacon and eggs sizzling in the pan on the cooker and the table laid for two.

'But where did the food come from?' she cried making no attempt to sit down at the kitchen table. 'I didn't leave much in the fridge because I am leaving. I would have gone yesterday if I hadn't been sick.'

'Sit down. You talk too much,' he told her, turning his back to give his attention to his cooking. 'Help yourself. There is orange juice and coffee. Do you feel like eating a cooked breakfast?'

She looked at the square shoulders and broad back, noting how the dark hair gathered in small curls on his neck. It was clear to her that he had the kind of body that made most women go weak just to look at him. The fact that she was already feeling weak from being sick did not help. There was a generous slice of honeydew melon on her plate and she spoke to him, not looking up.

'Just coffee and toast, please. I couldn't face anything greasy this morning,' she said huskily, and sat down very correctly in her chair.

'I went home to wash and change and collected the food from my apartment,' he said placing the food he had cooked on a plate he had warmed for the purpose. 'I hope you can bear watching me eat,' he added, carrying the plate to the table and sitting down opposite to her.

Sheena wondered whatever Dawn would have said to see them having breakfast together in her apartment and tried to believe, herself, that it really was happening.

'Very nice. I enjoyed the melon and the toast.' Sheena sipped her coffee and looked at him over the top of the cup. 'Where did you learn to cook like that?'

'I can do most things a bachelor has to do.' He finished the last portion of a perfectly cooked breakfast and put down his knife and fork on the empty plate. Then he reached for the coffee. 'I'm glad that you enjoyed your toast, but you won't get far on that. You did say that you were leaving?'

'Tomorrow. I would leave today, but I want to give the apartment a good clean up before I go so I will have to leave my departure until the morning.' She put down her cup. 'I hope I haven't inconvenienced you, but you shouldn't have come back this morning.'

'Like Mother Hubbard I saw that your cupboard was bare yesterday so I've stocked up your fridge and cooked breakfast. Listen, Sheena, why don't you try to get a job down here?'

'I can't get a job here and I don't want your charity. You can take that food back with you. I have quite recovered.'

'I can see that. You are back to your old sharp-tongued self.'

But Sheena knew that she would never be back to her old self again. Meeting him had set her off on far different channels from those she had been content to explore. He had put down his cup and was looking at her intently.

'If you mean I am being rude, you are wrong. I know that you have been very kind, but you would have done the same for anyone in a similar position.'

She wanted to yell at him to stop looking at her so intently. He had the most marvellous dark eyes, deep enough to drown in and her heart began to beat an erratic tattoo.

'Yes I would.' He kept looking at her again, just looking. 'Are you all right?'

'Of course I am,' she said crossly, wishing her heart would not frolic about.

He leaned back in his chair. 'Do you envy Dawn having this apartment?' he asked coolly.

'Envy her?' Sheena, taken aback, stared at him in utter astonishment. 'Good gracious, such a thing never entered my head.'

'That means you don't.'

'That means I do not.' There was a faint edge on her voice.

'You could have stayed here at no expense. Why don't you? Dawn told me you were a secretary. Have you been after employment here in London?'

'Perhaps I don't want to,' defensively.

'If you are good at your job you are robbing some harrassed business man of a good assistant.'

'That wouldn't be you, of course. I can never imagine you ever being harrassed at work. You have a perfectly clear idea of where you are going and . . . and.' She stopped with the feeling that she was living dangerously.

'Do go on,' he urged leaning forward with his arms on the table.

'I . . . I was going to say that I . . . wouldn't like to be in your way.'

He stood up, stretching to his full height, which Sheena judged to be over six feet, and began effortlessly, indifferently to gather the used dishes. Sheena bit her lip. She did not want him to wash them, to be indebted to him, so she said uncertainly, still with a glacial edge to her voice, as she rose to her feet,

'Please don't bother with the dishes. I can do them quite easily. If you will wait I will gather the food together that you have brought, I'll . . .'

Sheena got no further for he had grabbed her by the shoulders in a vice-hard grip. There was a whipping rush of anger in his voice.

'If you dare move one inch to that fridge you will be sorry for the rest of your life,' he challenged her darkly. 'I will not have my gift thrown back at me.' He glowered at her. 'Is it just me you are afraid of, or men in general?'

'Don't be ridiculous . . . please let go of me,' she said with far more calm than she had thought possible. The warmth of his hands scalding her skin presented a new and threatening element and she was horrified to discover that some elemental female response within her, was both repelled and drawn to it.

'Not so good in practice is it, this matter of setting out to protect a member of your family?' he said sardonically. 'You have to become involved in some dangerous situations, and you could have undertaken a job which is more than you can handle. You can dismiss me now that you have satisfied yourself about my base intentions.' His eyes narrowed. 'Or so you think.'

Sheena stared up at him, reminding herself that he might have full control of the situation, but that she had to maintain her dignity if nothing else.

With a strange gleam in his eye, a gleam which meant victory on his part, he complied with her request and released her shoulders. Then with a cool possessive movement which defied her to protest, he set his hands on her trim waist and drew her to him.

He smiled at the widening of her violet eyes and the tiny pulse beating rapidly in the hollow of her neck as he let her know by his expression what his intention was. His eyes had rested on her very inviting, partly-opened lips that trembled in dread anticipation. He brought his face nearer to hers.

'I can't make up my mind if you have been badly let down by some man in the past, or if it is jealousy of your sister and her success that makes you look and behave like this.'

Sheena winced inwardly at his gibes, but refused to let him torment her. Instead, with a tremendous effort of will, she spoke with a studied casual tone.

'I am surprised that I interest you enough for you to spend time reflecting on what makes me tick, but you are wasting your time. When you have finished manhandling me, perhaps you will go about your own business and let me go about mine?'

'I think this is known as stalling, isn't it? In other words, putting off the inevitable? But it won't, you know,' he murmured darkly.

'I am not stalling,' she contradicted him furiously.

He raised a dark brow. 'No? Then you have no objection if I continue?'

Sheena gritted her teeth. 'Get lost,' she hissed and pressed her hands against his chest, but they were imprisoned when his grip tightened. Silently and easily he mastered her attempts to free herself, drawing her soft curves tightly against his own hard body with a strength which left her breathless.

'How dare you?' she blazed wriggling with fury. 'I won't put up with this . . . this low rough play which evidently you are quite used to using on your women friends.'

'You have no choice in the matter,' he told her coldly, holding her tightly yet without hurting her.

Bitterly she told herself that he was well versed in such tactics as persuading his girlfriends to submit to his demands and by struggling she realised that she was inflicting harm upon herself from his hands. But she was not the kind to surrender without a struggle.

'You won't get away with this,' she panted angrily. Then his mouth was stifling any further protests from her lips as he crushed them into silence. For that first moment every bit of resistance she was capable of, rose against him. She heard him whisper her name, felt the room spinning round while he lifted her spirit above all earthly things, conscious only of him and his strength. It was unbelievable. His lips were taking something precious from her that would never be hers again. Her resistance melted like snow in the sun and complete surrender sent her arms creeping around his neck.

Gradually his kisses became more tender as he drank the sweetness of her lips. It was his deep chuckle of sheer masculine conquest that deafened her to the moan of esctasy that mingled with it—her attention whipping back to stark reality. All that had gone before came flooding back into her mind; all he believed her to be. She was a parasite, living off her younger sister, so why should she not be an easy conquest for him?

As he strove to hold her, she fought with blind, uncontrollable rage; wrenching herself free. She struck out until he caught her wrist and suddenly she was stilled under his enigmatic regard.

Unable to read what was in his mind, the rage within her died like an extinguished flame. 'Let me go,' she said weakly, her face pale and quivering.

He released her wrist at once, then swung round and left the apartment. It was quite some minutes before she was able to pull herself together and start to clear away the used dishes. All that day Sheena went around mechanically cleaning the apartment, refusing to allow her mind to dwell upon unsettling subjects like Ross Carlyle.

She had a cup of coffee at midday and made an omelette for her meal that evening. Her appetite had gone. The sickness of the previous day did not return, but she felt drained of all vitality. That evening towards eight o'clock her spirits wilted and she prepared tiredly for bed. A good night's sleep worked wonders and Sheena awoke the next morning feeling more able to face the day.

There were two trains leaving for the Midlands that morning and she decided to take the later one. The apartment was neat and sparkling, looking much brighter than she felt herself, she thought despondently. Her holiday was over and she was back to reality. She placed her large case in the hall and put the toiletries she had been using in the smaller handbag. The clothes Dawn had thrown out had been crammed in her bag.

She recalled with a pang Ross saying that she was jealous of her sister. Little did he know what a relief it was to her when Dawn managed to make a success of a job, the training for which Sheena herself had paid. She took a last look around the charming bedroom, lingering to look at her reflection in the mirror. The khaki linen safari suit with the little frilly white blouse and soft kid sandals could not have looked smarter. The high heels showed off her slender legs and fine ankles, but Sheena was not impressed.

Somehow the joy had gone out of her holiday. Maybe it was because Dawn had gone and the fact that she had no job to return home to. Well at least she would not have to buy any clothes for a while with Dawn's cast offs to help her out. The buzz of the doorbell startled her. It could not be her taxi because she had not telephoned for one yet.

Ross Carlyle stood in the doorway dressed casually in corduroy separates and an Italian cotton shirt that fell open at the strong brown throat. Sheena's first thought, after the initial shock, was of how tall, lean and handsome he looked. Her second thought was hardly complimentary at his sudden appearance on her door step.

'To what do I owe this dubious pleasure?' she asked icily, not asking him in.

His eyes took in her readiness to leave and then looked a little beyond her to where her case stood in the hall, then he cocked a brow.

'May I come in?' he requested.

'What for?' she said baldly. 'I haven't much time to spare. I am packed and ready to leave.'

'So,' said Ross airily.

'You and I have nothing to say to each other. My holiday is over and I shan't be sponging on Dawn any longer,' she went on grimly.

'Ouch!' He cringed in a dramatic way and arched a brow. 'You sling a barbed arrow,' he murmured. 'Look, I don't intend talking to you on your doorstep so, let me in.'

Taking a step forward he took hold of her arms and eased her gently back into the entrance of the apartment. Closing the door behind him he leaned back against it and surveyed her intently.

Moving uneasily beneath his scrutiny, Sheena blurted, 'I apologise for barging in on you uninvited that evening. I was rather worried about my part in the whole matter and I wanted to put things straight, but I . . .' She sighed and made a small hopeless gesture with her hands.

He scrutinised the soft rose colour flooding beneath her clear skin and smiled. 'I admire you for it. It took courage especially when you are frightened to death of me,' he said wickedly.

'I am not frightened to death of you,' she cried indignantly. 'Fear and dislike are very different.'

Ross looked her over in lazy appraisal, taking in her high colour, the lovely, wide, violet eyes and luxuriant auburn hair with gold lights in it like the tips of her long eyelashes.

'You can't dislike me all that much,' he drawled. 'You hardly know me.'

Sheena felt her face deepen in colour and she dropped her gaze to look at his well-shod feet.

'I don't want to know you,' she answered in a low voice.

'Why not?'

'I don't have to give a reason. What is it you want to speak to me about?'

'I refuse to discuss anything here in the hallway. Shall we go and sit down like two normal beings?'

She felt his fingers round her arm propelling her into the living-room and her heart responded wildly to that firm touch. His close virility was unnerving as she sat down in the nearest chair, avoiding the potential intimacy of the sofa. He chose the sofa, sitting in one corner and putting a long arm along the back. He was looking her over with an impersonal interest that brought anger up in her throat.

His drawl was almost insolent. 'For a girl who is returning home to no job we are in a mighty hurry.'

Sheena threw back her head and eyed him coldly. 'This isn't my day,' she said frostily. 'Another half hour and I would have been on my way home to no job, but at least with the considerable advantage of being away from you. Do tell me what you want to see me about, Mr Carlyle. Time and my patience are fast running out.'

He fixed her with the kind of look she imagined he gave to the more reluctant of his conquests. 'Is there anyone special you want to go back to? In other words can you please yourself when you go back?' he asked smoothly.

'Whether I have or whether I haven't has nothing to do with you,' she told him scathingly. 'If that is all you have to say, would you mind taking yourself off?'

He shook his head and gave her a wicked smile. 'That is what you are intending to do and you can't wait to get away. You aren't going back because your holiday is over. For you life is one long holiday until you find another job. Besides I bet that you haven't seen and done half the things you wanted to do here in London,' he told her reasonably. 'Here you have an apartment at your disposal . . .'

He broke off as something occurred to him and he

clicked his fingers disdainfully. 'Of course, it's the money angle isn't it? You have to be extra careful to make the money spin out now that you can no longer live off your sister.'

Instantly Sheena was on her feet shaking with anger, her violet eyes blazing at him.

'Get out,' she cried and made for the door.

He was there before her, barring her way. 'Well, well. At least we have a breath of honesty in your anger. You are indignant and rightly so because it has nothing to do with me how you make your way in life. On the other hand, though, it does disturb me to see a promising young woman taking the wrong path, because one never knows to what it might lead.'

Sheena drew in a deep breath, tinglingly aware of his nearness. 'Since this path appears to be on a crash course with yours, Mr Carlyle, the sooner I leave it the better. Now would you please go at once?'

'I could see you on the straight and narrow,' he murmured sardonically. 'It would be worth your while.'

Sheena gritted her teeth. 'You are in the wrong vocation. You should be in the Salvation Army, and I don't need saving . . . except from wolves like you.'

She did not care for the gleam which flashed in his dark eyes before it was extinguished by the narrowing of his lids.

'It could be that some of us might need saving from you.'

'You . . . you . . .'

The slender hand she raised to slap his face was caught in his steely grip and held there. A second later Sheena found herself hauled against him. Her first reaction to his kiss was utter astonishment. Her mouth, partly open, had been taken unawares by his sheer brute force. Furthermore the inherent passion in his kiss was contagious. His hand in the middle of her back held her firmly against him and his lips took a ruthless advantage of her helplessness. Sheena blamed her surrender on the suddenness of his attack, but she knew that there was something more lethal in his cruel embrace.

'So,' he said lifting his head to gaze down into her bemused eyes. 'I've proved that you can be aroused without even realising it, so I am sure I can cure you of your mercenary way of living off your sister. You could be quite a woman if you would let yourself go.' His firm mouth tilted into a hint of a ruthless smile. 'You enjoyed that kiss, didn't you?'

Sheena was still gasping for breath, trying to account for her reaction. He had kissed her with a deadly desire which she had never encountered even in her most amorous dates. He did not mean it and she must let him know that she was under no illusions where he was concerned. Kissing him was more heady than she could ever remember it ever being. Was it specifically because it was this particularly odious man holding her captive in his arms?

'You have the most over-inflated ego,' she gasped. 'I was too surprised to do anything. You are more contemptible than I thought—it's quite reprehensible to take advantage of a helpless woman.'

He grinned. 'You're not so helpless. I seem to recall that I was about to receive another blow from your dainty little hand. But really, Sheena, can you honestly tell me that you would prefer to go back to no job and a humdrum existence after what you have enjoyed here?'

Sheena pushed him away. 'Yes, I can,' she hissed through her teeth. 'Now will you please go?'

Ross eyed her thoughtfully, not touching her. 'But I haven't told you the real reason for my visit . . .'

'Forget it,' she cut in coldly, although she was still

trembling from his kiss. 'Nothing you have to say can interest me.'

He raised a tantalizing dark brow. 'Not even if it concerns your sister?'

'It can't possibly concern Dawn. She is out of your way now, thank heaven. I would be very happy if you would now get out of mine.'

'On the contrary. I can get Dawn back merely by crooking a finger.'

'You are bluffing, of course. You see, Dawn was adamant about marrying . . .'

She stopped in horror at her slip of the tongue, but it was too late. The expression in his eyes was unreadable and his voice showed no expression. 'What did you say?' he demanded.

'Nothing . . . absolutely—nothing,' she stammered. 'You have got me so confused that I don't know what I am saying.'

His eyes narrowed ominously. 'You are either a very clever woman or you are an inveterate liar.'

Sheena lifted her chin militantly. 'I am not a liar,' she cried furiously. 'All right, I'll tell you. Dawn is going to marry an American over in the States, so you see, you can't do anything about it now.'

Again that dark brow rose and he reached in his pocket for the letter Dawn had written. He tossed it on to the table beside her chair.

'Read that.'

She obeyed his command mechanically and picked up the letter. Sheena was not aware that he had walked over to the fireplace to turn and face her. Her eyes widened more and more as she read the contents of her sister's letter to Ross. Dawn made no mention of her fiancé. Indeed she gave Ross the impression that she was going to the States to fulfil a business engagement. She was keeping on the apartment in London until the end of the year because the lease had been paid up until then.

Dawn went on to say that she had to go in fairness to the people she worked for, but she hated leaving him. If he did want her to come back she would not hesitate. He had only to say the word. After all, Dawn had ended, 'I not only have an expensive apartment to keep up, but my sister is now out of work and I shall have to help her.'

Sheena was hardly aware of Ross speaking. She was so shattered by reading her sister's lies. It was not true. Dawn could not do this after all she had done for her. A dew of perspiration slicked her temples, and her hands holding the letter shook a little.

'Tell me, Sheena. Would you have delivered that letter if you'd known how much it condemned you? I noticed that you were in no hurry to give it to me that evening,' he said drily.

She moistened parched lips and refused to look up to meet his accusing eyes.

Huskily, she said, 'If I remember rightly, you were in no hurry to read it. In any case it isn't important—you and I will probably never meet again after today.'

'No? It seems I will have to put you in the picture.' He pushed his hands into his pockets and went on coolly. 'I had a proposition to put to Dawn before she left and you came into it.'

'I did?'

Sheena jerked up her head and gazed at him in bewilderment.

'That's right. I needed a person who could dress well and attend to my guests at business functions and I also needed a good cook. In the past I have engaged outside help for my parties and business dinners employing the self-catering people who prepare the refreshments and bring them along at the appointed time. However, as I have several very important dinners and parties to give I discussed the matter with Dawn.'

'With Dawn?' she gasped. 'But Dawn . . .'

'I know that Dawn is not exactly the hostess with the mostest, but she is very, very decorative and as my clients are business men . . . I'm sure you can see the drift of it.'

'I'm beginning to,' she murmured. 'But where do I come in?'

'Your sister assured me that you are an excellent cook, and that the two of you would work admirably together.'

Mechanically Sheena folded the letter and returned it to the envelope, then she put it on the low table where he had thrown it.

'I suppose I was meant to act as a chaperone in case Dawn demanded marriage from you,' she told him with an edge of sheer disgust in her tone.

'Marriage did not enter into it,' he replied softly with a hard gleam in his eyes. 'Dawn was to continue with her modelling in the day time and work for me in the evenings. I might add that I would only need someone to do this job for a matter of a few months.'

'And after that neither Dawn nor myself would be needed?'

'That's right.'

'All for your own convenience, no doubt. Well . . . now you will have to look for someone else. I might add that Dawn never mentioned anything of this to me. Not that it makes any difference. It only confirms my initial impression and suspicions of you. Once you had no further use for Dawn you would have dropped her like a hot potato.'

'She would have expected it, though, because I told her the job was only temporary.'

'How convenient for you. I'm sorry, but now you will have to look elsewhere for your staff.'

'Are you sure you wouldn't like the job?' he asked softly.

'I think I will forget you just said that,' she answered bitterly.

Unperturbed he looked at her intently. 'I want you to take on the job of both cook and hostess. Dressed in the right clothes, you could outshine Dawn and as a good cook you would know what to serve and when to serve it.'

'No way.' Sheena shook her head vehemently. 'You must be hard up for someone to do the job if you've had to resort to choosing someone you have accused of being both a scrounger and a liar.'

He shook his head. 'You don't understand. I know what type of person you are, but I still want you to fill the role I had in mind for Dawn. You intrigue me. I have to believe the evidence before my eyes. Even so, I might be able to change you into a different person. One who will stand on her own two feet instead of depending on someone else.' He half smiled. 'As I said before you have more fire than Dawn and in the right kind of clothes you could fill the role of hostess admirably.'

Sheena stared up at him in amazement taking in the wide shoulders and narrow hips in the well-made clothes. She recalled the impact of his kiss, the strength of his arms, the clean scent of his skin and the hard muscularity of his athletic frame. Men like Ross Carlyle did not go in for her kind. He preferred the sophisticated sort of woman who could play him at his own game and make it more exciting. He must take her for a fool.

She said stiffly, 'Don't tell me that you have a difficulty in finding someone to act as a hostess for you.

There must be dozens of women eager to fill the post since you are sure to provide all their clothes and there are good cooks in many agencies all over the country.'

He said slowly, 'You would think so, wouldn't you? Yet it isn't as simple as you seem to imagine. Women have an irritating habit of hanging around until there is no more money to lay their hands on. Secondly, they try all kinds of compromising situations in order to trap me into marriage.'

She said acidly, 'Some women are like that—they're the sort who'd go for anything masculine in trousers.'

'But not you?'

'That's right.'

He lifted wide shoulders. 'There, now you have the reason why I asked you to do me this favour. You don't like me, so there is no question of you trying to trap me into marriage. I will pay you well, but I shall expect you to work for it.'

'A kind of housekeeper-cum-hostess?' she murmured. 'To a woman out of work you dangle an interesting carrot, but I'm not hungry.'

'Do you think you will be hungry by this evening? I would like to take you out for dinner.'

'I'm afraid I shall not be here . . . which reminds me, time is getting on and I must be going,' she told him coolly.

'Running away?'

'From what?' she demanded loftily.

'From a perfectly sound offer of a job,' he murmured. 'I trust I don't have to resort to further persuasion.'

Sheena took a step back then halted—he would only say that she was afraid of him.

'It's time you left,' she declared firmly. 'I am not interested in any of your little games.'

'Ah, but this one is most interesting, because, you

see, I hold the trump card,' he said softly and moved a threatening step closer.

Sheena stood her ground. He was going to discover that she was not so easily intimidated.

'I'm not going to co-operate in your stupid mind games. It has nothing to do with me. Now will you please leave.'

'It does have something to do with me, because I could ask Dawn to come back.'

She swallowed on a dry throat, aware that his expression held a mixture of determination and ruthlessness. 'You mean you would send for Dawn, knowing that she will come if you lay on the charm enough. You would use her just like that when she has a chance of happiness with someone else in the States?'

'Why not? I'm not asking her to sleep with me and she will lose nothing by returning to London,' he answered mildly.

'But you know that Dawn is very attached to you and that her job as you call it, could easily end up with her doing some overtime in your bed. Of course that is a foregone conclusion.' She drew in an infuriated breath. 'You insidious, conniving devil,' she hissed. 'I could . . .'

'Yes?'

He raised an infuriatingly laconic brow, and she clenched her fists.

'Get out.' She controlled herself with an effort. 'Why you should pick on me I'll never know, apart from the lustful side of it and you have picked the wrong victim for your charms.'

'I don't think so,' he answered coolly, his look insolent and spellbinding. 'You have an untapped source of passion which intrigues me. Furthermore it is essential that I have a kind of rapport with any of my close associates, and strangely enough I find that I have it with you.'

'With me? You must be joking,' she cried.

'Are you so sure?'

Before she could answer, she was hauled into his arms and his mouth came down on hers with a sureness that was unmistakable. When he at last lifted his head, she was gasping for breath, unable to quell her own clamouring need for more. What was the matter with her. She hated him, didn't she? Was he right about her? He had certainly brought her to a height of passion she had never known kissing any other man. He was using all the trickery of which he was capable and she knew that she must not fall for it.

Slowly he released her eyeing her consideringly. Oh, he was very clever, she thought helplessly, but not quite clever enough.

'I think you had better go,' she said bravely. 'You and I have nothing more to say to each other. You can do what you like about Dawn. If she does come, I shall do my best to persuade her to have nothing to do with you.'

'Do you think that she will listen? Consider it carefully. You came to dine with me the other evening with a view to saving your sister from me. You came of your own accord. I am inviting you this evening. I shall call for you at seven and if you aren't here I shall know that your feelings for Dawn are as much a sham as you are. Think it over.'

CHAPTER FIVE

FOR a long time after Ross had gone, Sheena stood where he had left her, bemused and uncertain. The man was too full of his own needs and wants, and he was ruthless. In any case she considered him the wrong person for Dawn. It was easy to see what had swept her sister off her feet, though. He was different to other men. His good looks, charm and bold arrogance both excited and frightened a girl. Yet while she was preparing to leave the apartment his lean dark face kept coming between her and every task she did.

He evidently did not believe in love or marriage but his exciting appearance, his way of making a woman feel utterly feminine and attractive was proof that a girl's secret dreams could materialize into something real and lasting. He had admitted that she had made an impression upon him, that they had some kind of rapport . . . Sheena found herself in the kitchen with no recollection of having walked there. She had to make a drink.

Sitting at the kitchen table, drinking coffee, Sheena closed her eyes. Even the thought of Ross Carlyle filled her with an exquisite awareness, a sensation that could keep her here against her better judgment. Goodness! whatever was she thinking about? There was no way she was going to stay. Yet only a fool would turn down an offer of such a glamorous job, and she did not doubt for a moment that Ross would carry out his threat of sending for Dawn if he wanted to.

The coffee left in her cup was cold by the time Sheena

plucked herself from her thoughts and concentrated on the time. Her limbs seemed to be tied to the chair as the minutes ticked by and there was no quickening of her senses to know that soon she would be on the journey home. She looked around the neat, expensively decorated kitchen knowing that she would feel cramped in the one back home. The lovely freedom of high-ceilinged, light, airy rooms that were always lovely and warm with a flick of a switch to turn on the central heating made the idea of staying so attractive, but sadly, Sheena knew that she would soon forget the luxury here. All memories of her time in London would fade away, all except one—the dark, handsome face and the wide shouldered, loosely-moving figure of Ross. She would never forget him.

Dawn had not attempted to get in touch with her and she wondered how she was faring. She had evidently given Ross the wrong impression of herself, but she might have done it unwittingly. Ross was the kind of man who made one want to give a good impression. The afternoon found her wandering around the apartment unable to make up her mind as to whether to go home that day or not. Then as evening approached Sheena knew that she was going to stay overnight at any rate. She was crazy of course, but Ross had invited her, in her own right, this time and why should she not take advantage of his offer? At least she could pretend that everything was real, that he was an admirer who had invited her out for the evening. He owed her something for giving her such a bad time the last time she dined with him, albeit uninvited.

While she luxuriated in a perfumed bath, Sheena wondered if he would turn up as he had said. She had just the dress for the occasion, one which she had been fortunate to buy at a sale. In a beautiful shade of violet chiffon, it enhanced the same colour in her eyes heightening it excitingly. Drop ear-rings reflected the colour with a matching necklace.

As the time drew near for Ross to arrive she grew increasingly nervous. He arrived on the dot of seven o'clock, tall and menacing in his well-tailored jacket and narrow trousers.

'Aren't you going to ask me in?' he queried politely as she stood before him, tongue-tied and surprised.

'If you like,' she answered on a breathless note, hastening to open the door wide. 'Would you like a drink?'

'You mean before we go out?' he asked brushing past her into the entrance hall. 'I see that you are dressed, and very nicely too, for going out. I trust it's for our date?'

'Of course.'

With this, Sheena walked swiftly to the cabinet in the living-room where the drinks were kept and brought out a bottle of whisky. Pouring Ross a generous measure she managed not to spill it in spite of her trembling hands. She gestured to one of the comfortable chairs for him to sit down, her heart was pounding as she handed him his drink.

'Aren't you going to join me?' he asked stretching out his long legs. 'I hate to drink alone.'

She said awkwardly, 'There aren't many bottles left. There is some sherry and vodka. I was going to leave it in case Dawn comes back.' Reluctantly and not wishing to prolong an intimacy which set her teeth on edge, she poured herself a small sherry and sat down gracefully on a chair some distance away from him. The silence was charged with electricity.

'I decided to accept your offer to take me out for the evening,' she began. 'Look, Ross, can I be perfectly frank with you? If you do send for Dawn, would that mean that you might marry her?'

'Does that mean you have decided to accept my offer?' he parried, his dark eyes capturing hers as they sought to avoid him.

Sheena took a sip of her sherry to relieve a dry throat. 'You still haven't answered my question about Dawn. I want to know what you intend to do.'

He smiled swirling his drink round in the glass and spoke almost blandly, 'I think you know the answer to that one. Suppose we forget it and go out to eat?'

He tossed down the rest of his drink and Sheena did likewise then she was on her feet. As she reached for the silk evening jacket in a violet that matched her dress and trimmed with white fur, he took it from her.

'I trust you are going to relax and enjoy the evening?' he murmured against her ear as he helped her on with her jacket.

'I'd like to,' she confessed. 'I want to wipe out the memory of that other evening. It wasn't very pleasant.'

'You mean you would like the sort of romantic evening where your escort behaves like a gentleman and gives you a nice kiss on your doorstep?' he said, opening the door for her to pass in front of him.

'Not exactly. I wanted to be invited out instead of being accused of gatecrashing. You might not believe it, but I have never done anything like that before. I hardly think that I shall ever repeat it.'

'You don't have to resort to that. You are attractive enough to warrant plenty of invitations to dinner. Like your sister, you have the gift of making anything you wear look good.'

'Oh, come off it,' she cried, feeling slightly reckless. 'You were giving Dawn the hostess job and relegating me to the kitchen. You won't win me round with compliments.'

They were walking towards his car and she felt his

hand on her elbow. 'I have offered you both jobs,' he reminded her. 'I can't see why you don't accept.'

'I want a permanent job. One where I don't see too much of my boss.'

'What's that supposed to mean?' he asked, opening the car door for her to slide inside.

'As if you didn't know,' she scoffed slanting a grim look at him as she slid into her seat. 'Men can't keep their hands to themselves these days.'

'Doesn't that give you the opening to hook a rich husband?' he said moving around to his side of the car.

'Who wants that kind of a husband anyway? And don't get any ideas, because I may have decided to go out with you for this evening, but I am definitely going home tomorrow.'

'I've heard that before,' he mocked starting the car. 'I hope to change your mind.'

Sheena glanced at him from the corner of her eye as he started the engine and moved the car away. 'If you are expecting payment for the meal,' she told him, 'I can give you a cheque or cash. After all it's my last evening out and I would hate to be indebted to you. I think you owe it to me for the trouble you have caused.'

His deep voice held a hint of warning. 'All right, Cinderella, I'll be your Prince Charming for tonight. I hope you enjoy it.'

The restaurant Ross chose was an exclusive establishment with plenty of space between the tables thus giving one a chance of private conversation. Waiters drifted by noiselessly on the deep pile carpet juggling trays of delicious food and uncorking wine bottles amid the muted conversation of the diners.

'Well?' Ross asked sipping his drink and watching her over the rim of his glass. 'How is it?'

'Nice, but then you know it is. It is also heady.' The

wine slid down her throat, velvety and comforting to her taste buds.

'Is that a complaint?' he asked on a lifted brow.

'Of course not.' She lowered her eyes away from his teasing look wishing that he would stick to his more arrogant manner. He was easier to manage when he annoyed her and she was unprepared for this different aspect of his charade which he seemed to switch on at will. She took another sip of the wine feeling the need for the Dutch-courage it might instil. 'Are you still determined to send for Dawn if I don't consent to taking the job you offer?' she asked huskily.

'I haven't decided.' He paused contemplatively. 'I have a cook all lined up for a start. A very good one too I believe.'

Sheena's fingers tightened around her glass. 'You mean just for cooking?'

'Yes.'

Sheena decided to come to the point. 'What exactly are you planning to do? I think I have a right to know since it probably concerns my sister.'

'I told you, I hadn't quite made up my mind. Such a pity when you could make it up for me by being both cook and hostess, don't you think?' he answered as the waiter came.

She felt like throwing the contents of her wine glass all over him as he sat there with a smile on his well-cut lips and that eyebrow raised so tantalizingly. Her anger rose and she forced it back knowing that the only way to deal with him effectively, was to remain cool and indifferent to his taunting.

'I think Dawn will come,' he added for good measure and Sheena wondered how the plate of consomme would look adorning his shirt front.

'How can you be sure that Dawn will come?' she asked suspiciously.

'I've spoken to her over the telephone,' he replied and began to eat the clear soup.

She was shaking so much that her soup spoon was left beside her plate and she forgot her intention to remain cool. Her violet eyes sparkled with anger.

'Why you devious, malicious creature. I have a good mind to . . . to . . .'

'Yes?' he said unperturbed. 'I don't see what you have to be angry about. I've told you what I've done. I have been perfectly open with you. I asked for your help and you denied it so you can hardly blame me for asking Dawn.'

'You? Open?' she cried in a furious undertone mindful that they were in a public place. 'That has to be the most inaccurate statement of the year.' Sheena drew a deep breath, tightly between her teeth. 'Why you haven't given me time to consider, before you engage a cook. What is the reason for having me to dine with you this evening if you have already someone in mind for what you need.'

'Ah, I may have found a cook but you can still be the hostess if you want to, in Dawn's place. You have only to say.'

'Say?' she echoed. 'I couldn't eat with you. I'd choke. Goodbye, Mr Carlyle.'

She was on her feet when his arm shot out across the table and he had grabbed her hand.

'Sit down,' he ordered. 'You are attracting attention and I don't like to be unecessarily embarrassed. You will eat your meal and enjoy it. This is your splendid evening out and I mean it to be just that.'

Sheena felt her knees go weak at the grip of his hand around hers. Her quiver of panic was quickly growing into a fear of she knew not what. Sinking down into her chair as he released her hand, she said huskily, 'We can't carry on as if nothing has happened when we don't even like each other.'

Slowly Ross took in the shattered look on her face and her widened blue eyes.

'Even married couples who don't like each other manage to dine out together and look as if they are enjoying it,' he murmured with a mocking slant to his mouth. 'I don't know about you, but I am hungry.'

One delicious course after another was laid before them with Ross gradually taking on the role of the attentive and considerate host. He could charm when he had a mind to, Sheena thought with diminishing wrath.

'You should laugh more often,' he said when he had made her chuckle then burst into laughter at a very funny story he had told her. 'That husky laugh of yours is very sexy.'

'But I'm not a sexy lady,' she contradicted firmly.

It ws no use denying that he did affect her in every way. He managed to weave a disturbing sensation into the deep timbre of his voice until she wanted to move nearer to him and to know the thrill of his touch. By the time they had reached the coffee stage she felt happy and relaxed. The food had been excellent and his company stimulating. So much so that when he suggested that after they had finished they should go to a nightclub he knew, she agreed.

When she danced with him she felt a delicious sensation with the warmth of his hands sending exquisite ripples along her nerves. Neither of them seemed inclined to talk in the muted lighting. Sheena was trying to believe that all was well between them and that she was having an evening out with her favourite date. She closed her eyes and discovered a dryness in her throat, a sudden need. The realisation that she could really go overboard for her partner was enough to make her despair, for there could never be even friendship between them.

Sheena thought of Dawn and the possibility that she could be jealous of her own sister where Ross was concerned. It was ridiculous, but the mixture of emotions within her seemed to mock the fact that she no longer disliked Ross. Feverishly she reasoned that she was victim to his good looks and charm, the way he had of making a woman feel cared for and precious. Throughout their meal together, he had been solicitously attentive to ensure that she enjoyed everything. Of course, the wine could be blamed for the slightly giddy feeling she was experiencing at being so near to him.

Eventually she said, 'What did Dawn say when you got in touch with her? Did you mention me?'

He looked down at her searchingly for a moment and Sheena wondered what he was holding back. 'No. Your name was not mentioned by me, but Dawn did give me a message for you,' he admitted at last.

'You never said,' she began indignantly.

'You haven't given me the chance. I was going to tell you, but it didn't seem to be very important.'

Her violet eyes sparkled indignantly. 'Surely I am the best judge of that?'

'Actually it was nothing very serious. Dawn was anxious that you would have enough money by you until you get another job. She wanted you to know that she would help you if ever you were in a jam,' he said sardonically.

Sheena was shattered. Dawn who had never offered her a penny, who had even let her buy everything they needed in the apartment from food to cleaning materials since she had been there. The deep freeze had been empty when she had arrived on her holiday and it had been her money and shopping that had refilled it. Not that she had minded—she was having a holiday in a luxurious apartment free of charge and it was the least she could do to shop for provisions and do the cleaning and the laundry.

Presently she had gathered her composure enough to be able to say quietly, 'Why did you not think it important enough to tell me sooner?'

'Because I knew that if you were short of anything you would know how to go about getting it. After all, you have been living off your sister since she began to earn big money. You owe this holiday to her, do you not?'

Something inside her hardened, dispelling the inward fright of his presence and the numbness of discovering the game Dawn was playing. She wanted Ross to think well of her at someone else's expense . . . her own sister's.

Her first impulse was to cut and run before any more hurt came her way. Then the sort of stubbornness that had helped her in her desperate fight for Dawn's life when she had lain in the shadow of death for long, terrible, dark days, came to the fore. Sheena had always had to fight alone after their aunt had died and she could do it again. She would show Ross Carlyle that as a first rate cook and secretary she had no need to resort to asking her sister for help as Ross assumed she did.

'Terribly lucky, aren't I?' she scoffed. 'Is your offer of a job still open?'

'Why, yes.' He escorted her back to their table and seated her. Then he sat down opposite to survey her pale face with an intent regard. He did not intend to help her out and Sheena stiffened. She would show him, and he would not be giving all the orders either.

'I accept your offer, but only under certain conditions,' she told him, looking him straight in the eye. 'Suppose we hear your demands first, though?'

He frowned a little, a calculating gleam in his dark eyes. 'This is rather a sudden decision. I take it you mean that you want the job of hostess for the next six months?' he said drily. 'Incidentally, I didn't offer it to Dawn in our conversation.'

Sheena lowered her gaze on to his neat tie. 'I'd like to take on both the cooking and the entertaining side. It's a challenge I can't afford to miss.'

He regarded her quizzically in silence for so long that she felt inclined to scream.

'So, you accept the offer of the job, but only under certain conditions which you will give me only after hearing mine. What makes you think you have any right to call the shots?' he asked, his faint smile tinged with a touch of menace. 'I don't scare easily.'

'Neither do I,' she answered tartly.

'Well, as this is going to be a business discussion, I suggest that we go somewhere a little more private. Are you ready to leave?' He rose to his feet. 'We can go to my place since you are proposing to work for me.'

He had taken her arm in the firm grasp of his fingers when she paused to look uncertainly up at him. 'Isn't it a bit late to go visiting, or even to talk business?' she prevaricated.

'It's not too late for our kind of business,' answered her companion.

His apartment, she remembered, was not far from Russell Square, overlooking a small green park. He had told her that he had liked the attractive Georgian façade and had converted the suites of rooms on the top two floors into one interconnected, large, airy apartment while using the lower two floors as an office complex and guest facilities.

This time, because she was legitimately there as a guest, she didn't refuse his offer to show her around.

On the lower floor of his apartment a large living area occupied the entire length and breadth of the house, the windows at one end overlooking the garden. The dining-area and kitchen were at the other end. A spiral staircase, she remembered noticing it before, led up to his bedroom, he told her, and featured a massive skylight that opened up to allow access to the roof garden beyond. Sheena pretended not to hear his offer to show her his bedroom and made it plain that she was content to see the parts of the room that had been deep in shadow on her last visit to his flat.

'It's all so vast and splendid, in daylight you must get the impression of being surrounded by greenery from the roof garden and from the view through those lovely tall windows out over the park.'

His hand was gently persuasive. 'The views better from upstairs. I think you had better come and see the bedroom and the bathroom. You might have to use them sometime,' he murmured. He chuckled at the look on her face at his words. The soft amber glow of the wall lights picked out the clear cut lines of his dark face and highlighted the white gleam of his teeth as he grinned down at her. 'Only when I'm not here,' he added wickedly. 'Don't forget, the real reason I offered you the job and invited you here is because I know you will never try to compromise me.'

He followed her somewhat reluctant progress up the spiral staircase and eventually stood beside her in his bedroom. The roof garden through the skylight was plainly visible with the small floodlights hidden in the greenery. It would be a pleasant sight to wake up to every morning.

'No one to overlook, no one can see in here,' he said menacingly close by her ear as she turned her back on the king size bed.

The bathroom was concealed behind a wall which housed the built in wardrobes that faced the foot of the bed and which was the only break in the wide expanse of the room. 'I haven't shown you the guest bedrooms and bathrooms or my office and the boardroom, but they are situated on the lower two floors.'

As he spoke he walked easily down the spiral staircase and Sheena, somewhat bemused by the sheer size and luxury of the apartment, followed. As she made the final descent of the steps, she slipped, missing her footing on the narrow treads. Fortuitously though, Ross was waiting at the bottom and caught her as she fell. Sheena was bitterly regretting having agreed to work for him, she wondered what on earth had come over her. The work itself presented no problems, but Ross did. He affected her far too much and she grew towards him like a plant that yearned for the nourishing warmth and light of the sun. Now as she stood in his arms, she felt a flutter of fear at her own weakness within her breast.

'Sheena, palpitating?' he mocked as he felt the rapid beat with a hand over her heart. 'I don't believe it. Maybe we can make a real woman of you yet.'

She pushed him away. 'You mean the kind of woman you want me to be. The kind of woman who jumps easily into your bed? No thanks.'

He replaced his hands on her waist and their grip tightened ominously. 'If that were true, you wouldn't be safe with me now.' He bent his head and she stiffened, finding the aroma of his aftershave and the clean masculine scent of him overwhelming her resistance.

'Let's find out if you are as cool as you pretend to be.'

His dark eyes narrowed at the look of disgust and fear in her violet eyes then his gaze lowered to her pink lips that were partly open to show pearly teeth. Before she could say a word his mouth covered her own and he kissed her deeply and firmly. His arms were like bands of iron as the touch of his mouth effectively silenced any protest she might have made.

She struggled frantically, but her movements were mere wriggles against his hard lean body and it suddenly dawned upon her that it merely served to incite him. Trapped into capitulation, she discovered that his kiss was like dynamite to her sleeping emotions. The kiss was neither brutal, nor painful. At first it was exploratory savouring the sweetness of her soft lips, but when it deepened she experienced a riot of emotions which she had never believed existed in her.

Was this what the poets called real love engendered in the soul? Could it be possible that there was one special man who could take one to heights of happiness one could never know with any other? Sheena closed her eyes and when he raised his head her eyelids lifted to see the mocking look in his dark eyes. It stirred her like nothing else would have done and she stiffened. Instantly he released her. Her luxuriant auburn hair framed a face the colour of a red rose. Her violet eyes were wide with horror at the discovery she had made.

'Do you always find out the lay of the land when you employ new staff?' she managed with a fair amount of composure. 'You must see that I couldn't possibly work for you now.'

He raised a questioning brow. 'Why not? I assure you I am perfectly safe as an employer,' he reassured her. 'I have already stressed that I want no trapping into matrimony. What's in a kiss anyway?' He smiled wickedly. 'It was only an exploration.'

Sheena was feeling steadier on breath regained and her eyes widened in disbelief.

'Is that what it was? You could have fooled me. Maybe that's what you are planning to do,' she retorted angrily. 'To have a mistress, a cook and a hostess all in one. On the cheap.'

He gave her a look that was meant to cut her down to size. 'So you think I'm the kind of man who would resort to every mean trick in the book in order to be a success? Well, what about it?'

'What about what?'

His hands were on her shoulders, drawing her to him. 'You might as well go the whole hog and be my mistress as well.'

Sheena began to pull away by placing her hands on his wide chest.

'You have to be joking,' she said in disgust.

'You put the idea into my head. You can only blame yourself for my agreeing.'

His arms were deceptively loose around her and as they tightened Sheena was determined not to demean herself this time by struggling against his superior strength.

'I didn't come here to play games, Ross Carlyle,' she said huskily. 'Will you please let me go?'

To her chagrin she was unable to stiffen her body against him because his grip was so tight. She was crushed against his hard muscular frame and his mouth was forcing its way on to her tremulous one. The demanding kiss seemed to be never ending until the harshness changed into something that was sweet and wonderful. Gradually her body was filled with a seductive warmth and her arms crept around his neck as their bodies merged into one pulsating column. She had reached the point of complete surrender when Ross lifted his head and released her.

The sudden descent from the heights of esctasy was almost too much for Sheena, and she gazed up at him in bewilderment with wide luminous eyes. Her face was a warm rose colour, her pink lips tremulous and bruised by his kisses. A gleam came into his dark eyes which was quickly dampened as he coolly scanned her features.

'And now perhaps we can talk about what we really came here for,' he said without much expression.

Shattered by the treacherous response of her whole being to his kisses, Sheena made no demur when he led her into the seating area of the spacious lounge. How he despised her, she thought shakenly. He would never have treated her so contemptuously had he respected her. Well she would show him in her new job, that she did not have to resort to asking anyone to support her. She had taken a course in Domestic Science and as a result was a first class cook. When Sheena Denton had finished with him he would wonder what had hit him. Working for him would equip her with more experience and she would come into contact with influential people who would help her to find a good permanent position.

He guided her to a sofa decorated by pretty coloured cushions at the end of the room that overlooked the garden. The soft golden lamplight made the room seem smaller and shadowy and he took a seat not far away from where she sat but in the half shadow.

'A drink before we talk?' he suggested with a raised brow.

'No thanks.'

He evidently did not need one since he made no move to get a drink for himself. She moved uneasily wanting to get everything over and done with and make her escape.

'Shall we begin with discussing the offer you made me?' she said bitterly.

He watched her for a second, then lowered his dark gaze to his well shod feet stretched out before him. When he spoke he did not look at her.

'Which one, the hostess or the cook?' It's obvious that you don't want Dawn to come back to act as hostess.'

'I want to take both jobs,' she said, and his eyes rose to meet hers. She was at a loss to read the expression in his intent gaze. It was no use for her to look too far ahead to the times when she would be in his company to face similar incidents like the one that had just occurred. If she allowed herself to delve deeper into awkward situations which were a distinct possibility when once she was in his employ Sheena knew that she would become more than a little afraid.

'Think you can manage them both?' he queried. 'I shall expect a high standard of your culinary skills. As for the hostess part, I am sure you can take that in your stride. Dawn would have perhaps been the perfect hostess because she has been trained to make clothes look good on her lovely figure.' He looked her over. The soft golden light played an aura around her luxuriant hair turning it to fire. Her lovely violet eyes were wide with interest as he talked, and Sheena was sure he had not missed an inch of her curves from top to toe. 'On the other hand your sister is lacking in your spontaneous warmth and fire. You could be quite a woman with a little bit of training,' he added wickedly.

Her face was flooded with warm embarrassed colour—they both knew that he was alluding to her surrender just now to his kisses.

'When a woman has been wined and dined she might be led into forgetting herself and responding to anyone's advances, and you did order a very heady and intoxicating wine. Unfortunately for me I am no drinker,' she protested.

He chuckled at this. 'Fine,' he jeered. 'I won't have any worries about you drinking all my whisky.' He looked again at the beautiful dress, the tantalizing glimpse of her youthful breasts between the opening of her plunging neckline, the trim waist and image of her long lovely legs which she had crossed from the knee beneath the folds of her gown. 'I shall insist upon buying your clothes, of course. For the entertainment side.'

Sheena bridled. 'That is what I meant when I said I have conditions as well as you. I don't want you to buy my dresses. I have enough of my own.'

His dark eyes narrowed suddenly wary in this, the first battle of wills. 'I shall insist upon seeing them.'

His words were curt and his tone was disapproving. She surmised that he liked to be the piper who called the tune.

She said sweetly, 'You mean that you doubt whether I have the kind of money to purchase really chic things? You needn't worry. Dawn had unloaded almost her entire wardrobe of last year's dresses and suits on me.'

Surmise what you will from that, she thought. You've already accused me of living off Dawn, so here's proof for what you want to believe.

His dark eyes held a strange glint. 'I hardly think that they will be suitable for what I have in mind,' he remarked drily. 'Your clothes go with the job.'

'I wasn't thinking of wearing them. I intend to take them to someone who will give me a good price for them and with the proceeds I can buy what I need. I am quite good at using separates to get a first rate effect.'

He frowned. 'Separates?' he mocked.

'Tops and skirts. When one has a limited budget one learns to buy few things of good quality and mix and match.'

Ross said angrily, 'I don't want any made up things. I insist upon providing you with a decent wardrobe.'

'Like my cooking, Mr Carlyle. I can make quite a stir if I put my mind to it,' she quipped bravely.

He said slowly, his tone dangerous, 'You might think that you know all there is to know about entertaining, the right food, the exact clothes and so on, but I have had more experience with such things than you could ever get in a lifetime. I am older than you and I know what I am talking about.'

'I can match you move for move,' she challenged furiously.

'Fine as long as you admit it when you are beaten and act accordingly instead of running away. I shall be around most of the time at first to help you.'

'I thought that I was supposed to be helping you,' she said sarcastically.

He said curtly, 'Sometimes you can help more when you co-operate with the one you are supposed to be helping.'

'Meaning that you want things done your way?' Sheena cried indignantly. By now she could not wait to get away and she rose abruptly to her feet. 'I think I would like to go now and think it over,' she murmured quickly.

'Yes, go on—chicken out now that the going's getting rough. Is that what you are proposing to do in your job?' he jeered and rose to his feet in one agile movement. Suddenly he was there right in front of her. 'Aren't you forgetting something, Sheena?'

'Like what?' She stepped back, but he advanced upon

her, his eyes perusing her flushed face, the pulse beating in the hollow of her neck and the tantalizing shadow deep in the cleavage of her bodice. He had said earlier that this was to be a romantic evening for her and that he would kiss her good night. The mere thought of it left her speechless with alarm. Once in his arms her defences were as fragile as egg-shell, easily crushed by the strength of his arms and the magic of his kiss. Against her reasoning will she found her eyes drawn to his firm sharply defined mouth.

'You haven't asked what your salary will be and I know you are interested in that,' he said mockingly. 'I'm giving you a month's pay in advance. Everything you buy for the apartment, food and other things I want you to put down to my account.' He gave a wicked smile and raised that aggravatingly mocking dark brow.

'Is there anything worrying you? You've gone quite pale,' he said and her gaze fell from his mouth in her embarrassment.

The worm, she thought angrily. She could see that he knew she had been thinking of that promised romantic end to her evening out with him—the kiss he had said would round it off. He had meant her to think about that.

Anger stiffened her defences. 'It could be that I am overwhelmed with the thought of so much money,' she scoffed. 'You know how greedy I am for anything thrown my way now that I am no longer able to sponge off my sister.'

Her violet eyes met his gaze with scorn. The gleam in his dark eyes changed to one of speculation. 'I don't believe you,' he told her softly lifting her chin with a firm finger. 'This is really what is worrying you, isn't it?'

He laid his mouth on hers in a firm kiss. 'There, that

is all it was going to be,' he said as she drew in a much needed breath. 'Any more conditions?'

'Yes,' she hissed. 'Under the circumstances I think it will be better if I stay in Dawn's apartment for the six months I am to work for you . . . and there's to be no more kissing.'

His kiss had kindled a fire that raged through her at his touch. It was only too easy to forget how much he despised her and to give way to the demands of her body. It was all so confusing, she told herself unhappily.

'I am afraid that can't be managed at the moment. You see there will soon be occasions when I am entertaining and my parties often stretch into the small hours. I could not allow you to leave so late for your apartment. It won't always be convenient for me to take you there.'

He had pushed his hands deep into his pockets and was surveying her coolly. He was too close to Sheena for her to forget the demanding strength of his embrace and she quivered inside at the thought of his kisses. There was so much about him that disturbed her, the musky aroma of his aftershave, the firm leanness of his body as it crushed against her and the heaven of being held in his arms. She felt such pleasure in his company, and grateful for his being around now that Dawn had gone.

Sheena took a grip on her emotions. There would be no love for her from Ross Carlyle. She was not his kind of woman. He obviously preferred long-legged, sophisticated blondes like Dawn. Why did she have to keep thinking of Dawn and her part in all this? she admonished herself.

'I see your point,' she agreed, thinking that while his bedroom was above the living-room hers would be one of the guest suites far enough away from his lair for her to fall prey to his demands.

'I'll give you a cheque in advance.' He broke in on her thoughts to offer her part of her pay and held out a pre-written cheque. 'Come on, take it. It won't bite.'

Sheena stared in amazement at the amount he had written down. 'An advance?' she croaked. 'It's far too much money for that.'

'You are going to do at least two jobs,' he reminded her. 'If you are going to work for me you will have to learn to accept my terms.'

His tone made her bridle. 'And you have to accept mine,' she retorted.

'That's fine by me so long as they are fair conditions. I would like a trial run though, if you don't mind?'

Sheena stared at him uncomprehendingly. 'I don't understand?'

He was eyeing her with an expression that she could not define and it worried her, even though it patently held no visible threat.

'Come and cook me a meal tomorrow evening when you have stocked the freezer and cupboards. We can put on a show, a rehearsal for when I really entertain guests.'

'Here?'

'That's right.'

'I trust that it won't run into the small hours like your "real" parties. I want to be able to return to my own apartment.' she said coldly.

'Oh, yes. Now . . . tomorrow we shall go shopping . . .' He put up his hand to silence her as she was about to speak. 'I shall go shopping with you, to ensure that your choice of clothes meets my requirements.'

'Oh, no, you won't. I am quite capable of dressing

correctly,' she snapped.

'Let me remind you that some of my guests will be business men from the continent,' he said with an unexpected abruptness. 'There could be a lot at stake in terms of business acumen when I entertain them, so good impressions are of paramount importance.'

'Really?' she mocked. 'As I said before. I don't frighten easily. I think that they will be suitably impressed by my own choice of wardrobe.'

'I certainly hope so. By the way, I have a daily help who comes in each morning to clean for me. She can cook too, but not the kind of dishes I shall require. That is where you come in.'

'Did you trick your daily into working for you, like you did me?' she asked sweetly.

'I wouldn't say that I have tricked you, merely that I persuaded you to see what a good offer it is,' he said with a half smile.

'You needn't look so pleased.' Sheena had taken the cheque and was slipping it into her purse. 'I think I have the measure of your needs and I am used to fending off men. I was doing it every day in my old job,' she told him with spirit.

An evening alone with him in this beautiful apartment was not going to be so bad so long as he understood that there were not going to be any gratuitous handouts on her side.

It was impossible for her to read the meaning in the sudden gleam in his dark eyes. It could have been admiration or something far more dangerous. Later in her bed that night, Sheena wondered which was going to be the bigger challenge, the responsibility of her job or coping with Ross Carlyle. Indeed against his virile maleness and the strains it imposed upon her the demands of the job would be small potatoes. She glanced towards the table by her bed on which reposed the bunch of spare keys he had given to her to his apartment. They seemed to gleam at her threateningly in the dim light.

CHAPTER SIX

At nine-thirty the following morning Ross arrived to take her shopping in a car that was long, streamlined and svelte—it suited his overall image. He pushed the trolley round the supermarket and carried the boxes of goods to the boot of his car with effortless ease. He appeared to be unaware of her surreptitious scrutiny of him on these occasions.

He did not have to be so good-looking, Sheena thought peevishly, as she glared at the neat, black, curly hair, the lean, tanned features, the casual well-cut cinnamon trousers, cream shirt and hand-made, leather shoes.

He had made it plain that he was pleased with her appearance, for he had grinned admiringly when he had picked her up at her apartment. She had used her flair for clothes to the best advantage. The striped cropped trousers in an Aztec pattern of orange, red, green, and brown, showed her shapely legs and the matching mandarin-necked, three-quarter sleeved top enhanced the beauteous length of her slender neck.

He had loaded the last case of Scotch in the car boot when he suggested that they call somewhere for a drink. The whole morning had been like a dream to Sheena as they had gone shopping looking for all like any married couple. But this was a purely business deal and she told herself that she must not forget it. So she remained cool and concentrated on reading her list of requirements with occasional smiles and nods at her companion. At least he would see that she was no greenhorn when it came to shopping for special catering.

The coffee shop was in a tiny courtyard behind the main shopping parade. Lots of brightly coloured geraniums in tubs brightened the cobblestones, and striped coffee and cream canopies were draped over the quaint bow windows and doors. The interior of the café was dim and cool and Sheena was glad to sit down and rest her aching feet by slipping off the dainty high-heeled sandals. Ross had guided her to a table overlooking the miniature courtyard and she noticed how the waitress looked at Ross admiringly when he gave the order. His ready smile had flashed out at the woman and treacherously Sheena wished that he would look at her like that.

Mostly his interest in her had been purely speculative. She also had the feeling that his every action was guarded where she was concerned. He was an intriguing man, but she had no intention of becoming emotionally involved with him. She would have to stay on her toes in order to handle him, but she would try to do her best. Perish the thought that she might become as cynical as he was, however.

The coffee was good and she sipped it savouring the mellow, sweet blend, unaware of the interest she was drawing from a woman at the next table who had already risen to leave.

'Sheena,' she cried coming forward to stop at their table. 'I thought you had gone back home after Dawn left for the States?'

Sheena's violet eyes narrowed as she looked up at the newcomer in an effort to put a name to her vivacious face. The woman helped her out.

'Have you baked any good pies just lately? Gosh, I never remember going to a party when I enjoyed myself so much. Remember me, Jacqui Frost, the girl who wolfed down your delicious cooking at Dawn's final fling. I still dream about those patties and sweets.'

Sheena gave an embarrassed laugh. 'You were probably hungry,' she teased. 'I'm glad you enjoyed them. As for me I have decided to stay on for a while in the apartment.'

Jacqui looked at Ross with one of those glances that seemed to take in every feature of his amused face.

'Lucky you,' she guffawed giving her attention once again to Sheena. 'I don't blame you for staying one little bit. Don't forget I am still around if you do any entertaining. Nice seeing you again. Have to dash. Goodbye!'

'You made an impression there,' mocked Ross when the woman had gone.

'My baking,' laconically. 'I did all the food for some of Dawn's parties.'

'So you *can* cook,' he said mildly, although the expression in his eyes gave her no quarter. 'Frankly I wasn't expecting anything great from you this evening in the way of a meal. But now you had better watch out, because I am expecting wonders.'

'The world is full of little surprises, isn't it?' she answered and sipped her coffee. 'For instance, if anyone had told me that you and I would be shopping this morning, I would never have believed them. And while we are on the subject of little surprises, don't expect me to account for every minute of my time when I am not on duty.'

He raised a curious brow. 'You know something? Life is becoming quite interesting again. Remind me when we return to my apartment, to show you my wine cellar.'

Ross had unloaded all the shopping, putting the drink crates in the hall until everything else had been put away. Then he proceeded to take the cases down to the wine cellar in the basement, below the suite of offices. When he had finished stacking the bottles he returned with a bottle of wine and put it in the refrigerator for the evening.

'Would you like to come down to the wine cellar with me? he asked Sheena, who was in the kitchen going through the items she would need for the evening meal.

She would have preferred to explore on her own, but refusal would have betrayed her cowardice. She faced him bravely, wondering at this late hour whether she had better back out. Never in a million years would she ever get used to his vibrant presence. A quiver ran through her at thinking what a wonderful lover he would be. She shivered.

'What's wrong?'

Sheena came back to earth suddenly aware that Ross was eyeing her with concern.

'Nothing . . . er . . . I think I shivered in anticipation of the chill in the cellar,' she babbled. 'Right, show me the way to your basement.'

They were going down the stairs and he was leading the way. Sheena looked down at his wide shoulders and the curly tendrils of hair lying neatly against his shirt collar. She was becoming obsessed with the man. It was the result of being in his company too much, she guessed. Thank goodness that after this evening she would be in the kitchen, cooking or preparing for one of his dinner parties while he was out of sight entertaining his guests. She could not resist a tiny pause as they went past his office on the ground floor. There was no sound of a typewriter.

He did not miss a thing. 'My staff aren't working at the moment. They have this week off,' he said as he turned to open the door that lead to the cellar. 'You will notice that there is a platform here as you enter to save anyone rushing in thinking it is a room and dashing headlong down the stairs.' He opened the second door after switching on the lights down below. 'Take your time, the stairs are steep.'

In the cellar the lights shed a golden glow on the rows of shelves that housed the bottles. Ross had placed an arm around her shoulders as he pointed out the different years and types of the wines and spirits.

'You don't ever need to come down for anything. I will get whatever you want for you,' he told her and squeezed her shoulder.

He was much too close and Sheena found difficulty in breathing. With an abrupt gesture she shrugged off his arm pretending to a desire to look at the thermometer on the wall. She gazed at it unseeingly and quelled a shiver at the chill around her shoulders where his arm had lain. It was that sudden feeling of coldness and loss that drove home to her how close she was coming to losing her heart to him. No use telling herself that the feeling had been there from their first meeting; that deep down she had known the truth all along.

Ross had come behind her. His warm breath was on her hair as he placed a hand on her shoulder.

'This is an excellent place for keeping everything in tip top condition,' he said.

Sheena felt a sudden urge to get away from his nearness. She turned and found herself up against him. In the muted light he seemed to be massive and when his arms whipped around her she wanted to scream. There was no one in the house but the two of them and there was nothing to prevent him taking her upstairs to his bedroom and having his way with her. And she, poor fool, would not have the will to resist him.

One half of her was loathing him and the other was telling her how wonderful it would be to succumb. It was not as though he had any romantic leanings towards her. He had her there to suit his purpose.

She leaned back in his arms as her eyes locked with his.

A torrent of emotions swept through her and she sought frantically for something to say to cut the tense atmosphere which was tearing her apart.

'Sorry,' she gasped pushing against his hold. 'You never said if you were wanting lunch here? I take it my duties do start from now?'

He made no attempt to release her but smiled sardonically at her efforts to remain cool.

'Don't be in such a hurry,' he murmured drawing her closer. 'You know, I think we shall make a real woman of you yet. You are really quivering like a bird or is it all part of the act?'

He pulled her back into his arms and crushed her opposition with a breath stopping kiss. Sheena struggled violently at first then the magic seeped through and she moved nearer to his hard frame. Her hands crept upwards, lingering on the wide shoulders, but before they could fasten around his neck he drew away.

'That was some act you put on,' he said curtly his dark eyes narrow and hard. 'I hope you aren't getting any ideas of using me as your new pay packet?'

Shaken as much by his kiss as by his unjust accusation Sheena felt her anger being submerged by his contempt for her. He did not know anything about her really except what he chose to believe.

'You are my new pay packet, but I shall only take pay for the services I give. Let us get one thing clear, though. I am only doing the two jobs assigned to me—any others are out. I think you know what I mean. I would also like to meet the lady who comes in to clean before I begin my duties.'

He released her slowly. 'Rita Clarke, my daily help

has the day off today. You will like her. So I presume that you are taking on the position?'

Sheena nodded without enthusiasm. 'Against my better judgment, perhaps. I am going to prove to you that I am not the kind of a person you seem to think. Like you I enjoy a challenge. No woman is entirely dependent on any man. In my opinion women do most jobs better.'

He gave a half smile. 'That's interesting,' he murmured on a half smile. 'Do you think that you could rustle up some lunch for me without putting arsenic in it?'

'Don't tempt me,' she hissed and made for the cellar steps.

'You surprise me,' he scoffed. He was much too close behind her. 'I thought you were doing the tempting.'

Sheena was already up the stairs and going very quickly to the living quarters. If she had ever had any hope of her romantic ideas coming true with a man like Ross Carlyle, she would certainly forget them. He had accused her of putting on an act and of being a phoney all through. She would never forget that.

Soon Sheena had forgotten her anger in doing a job she loved—cooking. In her white overall with a matching band around her hair she served up his lunch on the hot hostess wagon and wheeled it in. Ross rose from a chair and put down the newspaper he had been reading. He quirked a brow at her clinical appearance and smiled crookedly as he strode to pick up the bottle of wine he had put at the ready.

'You are joining me, of course,' he said as the cork popped and he filled two glasses.

Sheena turned to leave the room. 'No,' she answered. 'I have things to do.'

'You will come and sit down,' he ordered. 'I am sure

that as a good cook, you will want to witness my enjoyment of your culinary skills?'

She went back into the kitchen and slipped the band off on her hair and removed her overall. Then she combed her tousled locks and returned to the dining area. A shiny nose did not bother her, for she was past caring how she looked to him.

The hot crisp pancakes filled with cooked soft cheese impregnated with herbs were delicious. So was the turbot covered with a delicious sauce. The succulent slices of cold ham cooked in honey went well with a crisp salad followed with cheese and biscuits. Ross ate his share with obvious enjoyment and he rose at the end of the meal with alacrity to make the coffee.

If Sheena had been surprised to find that he had already laid the table when she had wheeled in the trolley, she was even more surprised to see him deftly put the used dishes on to the trolley before taking it to the kitchen. All through the meal he had turned the conversation to the art of cooking and she had been drawn out to speak of her love for it. They had almost called a truce and she was left sipping the last of her wine before he came back with the coffee.

He received a suspicious look from beneath her thick eyelashes as he entered. She refused to believe that he was helping out of kindness. To her way of thinking he was trying to prove that he, as a man, could do as well as she could. He had virtually forced her into taking the job and he had forced kisses upon her that were more or less insulting, since he had nothing but contempt for what he believed was her way of life. No, even the devastating combination of good looks, charm, dry wit and virility failed to stir her now.

He poured out the coffee, remembering that she preferred it white and sat down to lift his cup in a salute.

'To a very enjoyable meal,' he said. 'I drink to your culinary abilities. If all your meals are like the one we have just eaten, I shall have no complaints to make. As I said before life is full of surprises.'

'I couldn't agree more,' she said sweetly and lifted her cup.

Sheena prepared a four course meal for that evening. As far as she could gather there was to be just the two of them, Ross and herself. With everything ready—all but the last finishing off—she went to take a bath and choose something to wear. The cream, brown, beige and blue striped skirt had a draw string waist and the cream and gold shot top with its slashed neckline showed off her youthful figure to perfection. The blue and gold striped cummerbund was fringed at the ends and emphasised her trim waist. Her gold loop earrings added a sophisticated look to a very modern outfit.

Later when she sauntered into the living-room to tell Ross that the meal was ready, Sheena was wishing that the evening was over. The meal did not worry her. Everything had turned out right and it was cooked to perfection. She had included game in the courses and several items which lifted an ordinary meal into a gourmand's feast.

'A sherry?' Ross turned glass in hand to glance at her then to take her in more fully. 'You look Bohemian and very beautiful,' he said.

'I am Bohemian remember? I scratch a living where I can from others,' she murmured accepting the sherry and eyeing him beneath her lashes. 'The meal is ready to be served.'

That evening was the happiest Sheena knew she would ever have. Ross took a hand in serving the courses and again he made the coffee. During the meal Ross had questioned her as to how much she had seen of London.

'There's a lot you haven't seen,' he told her after she had described the sights and sounds of her holiday. 'I might take you around myself if I have the time.'

Sheena had no intention of going anywhere with him, however. She drank the coffee too quickly and almost scalded her throat. There followed a spasm of coughing during which Ross handed her his handkerchief.

'You can't wait to get away, can you?' he said sharply.

'There are the dishes to wash,' she answered, putting down her cup and handing back his handkerchief.

'If that is what is worrying you, we can do them now.'

'But . . . you don't have to do them,' she stammered. 'I am quite capable of doing a few dirty dishes. There are no pots and pans because I clean them as I go along.'

'Then it won't take us long to do them, will it?' Ross rose to his feet, collected the coffee things and strode into the kitchen.

Sheena followed him and in no time at all he was turning on the hot water. The job was carried out in silence with Sheena wishing there was somewhere to go to as an excuse for getting away from him. The day had all been so unreal she had felt rather like a married woman after spending the day shopping and eating with him. All that was needed was for them to climb into the same bed. She had put herself into an unfortunate position. She was at his mercy and he was playing it out for all he was worth. He knew that he had her on tenterhooks wondering about his next move. When they returned to the lounge, she was determined to make an excuse at the first opportunity to retire to her room.

To her dismay he guided her to one of the long sofas and gently pushed her down on it. Then he sat down beside her. He half-turned with his arm at the back of the sofa and Sheena had her glance towards him trapped by his cool enquiring dark eyes. There was no particular warmth in them when he spoke.

'Well it has been a very successful day, don't you agree?' he asked. 'I am sure that you will suit me nicely.'

'So I am to be given a reluctant go ahead for the present. Is that it?' she said coolly, although her heart was beating madly in her breast.

Her gaze slid away from the amusement glowing in his eyes. His nearness unnerved her and it made her mad to know that he was aware of it.

'What do you mean, for the present?' he drawled. 'We can get along very well together if you would just let yourself relax. Suppose we kiss and make up? You need me and I need you. So let us enjoy our time together, it will be all too brief. Pleasant interludes always are.'

His fingers began to caress the back of her neck and she sat up stiffly, leaning away from his hand.

'I don't usually kiss my employers for accepting me on their staff,' she cried with spirit. 'And keep your hands to yourself. You can do that kind of thing with women of your own kind.'

'And what is my kind of woman?' he asked softly dropping his hand behind her to her waist. 'Don't forget that Dawn was on my list.'

'Which was why I got her away.' Sheena tried to rise to her feet and found his arm around her waist pinning her down.

Then next moment he had scooped her up across his knees imprisoning her arms with the grip of the arm around her back. She was quivering, helplessly at his mercy as his head came down and his mouth moved tantalizingly over hers. The small sound of protest coming from her lips was muffled then stilled altogether by the deepening pressure of his kiss. The beat of her heart in the silence of the night seemed to deafen her. But it was the sweetness of his lips which finally killed any resistance left in her.

She could feel her body sinking into the warmth and hardness of his, and gradually a feeling of utter bliss washed over her.

'Has no man ever made love to you before, Sheena?' he whispered against her lips. 'Or did someone let you down badly? Those slumbering fires inside you are quite banked up. Are you going to let me help you to release them?'

If Sheena could have spoken she would have told him that he already had. Already her body was clamouring for his touch. But a growing inertia left her lying passive in his arms as he savoured the sweetness of her lips in deep, moving kisses. It was the possessive caress of his hand moving from her back to her hip which finally roused her to the danger. She almost groaned at the weakness of her own body defences at his touch. With a strength she had not known she possessed, she squirmed in his arms, gasping for breath as he released her.

Swift as she was, he reached the door before her, barring her way. His face was set as he gripped her shoulders and shook her slightly.

'Calm down,' he told her sternly. 'What's in a kiss anyway? You aren't a child and I am a grown man. For heaven's sake, I haven't taken you to bed with me. This is purely a business proposition.'

'And do your business propositions include sordid bedroom games?' she demanded scornfully with the rapid rise and fall of her firm breast showing her agitation. 'If they do, then get someone else to do your entertaining and cooking.'

There was no softening in his dark eyes as they raked

over the trembling of her lips and the hatred in her wide violet eyes.

'I assure you that I wasn't playing any game. I was trying to discover the real you beneath that cool façade that you use to cover up a scheming mind,' he said grimly, dropping his hands from her shoulders. 'I will take you to your room on the floor below and I will bring your belongings here when you have packed at a time to suit yourself.'

She stalked out in front of him as he stepped politely aside and they went downstairs. It was no use, she told herself. Ross Carlyle was the type of man who enjoyed emotionless, sexual affairs which he could leave behind with no regrets. His charm and masculinity were dedicated to this kind of life and she was not going to make any difference to it.

When she stepped into the bedroom he had allotted to her the pleasant surprise it gave her swept aside her former anger at his behaviour. The deep cream wool wall to wall carpet was complimented by magnolia walls with a turquoise bed spread and lamps with matching turquoise shades. There was a telephone beside the bed and built in cupboards along with a spacious wardrobe. A television, writing desk and small book case with several white wicker chairs upholstered in cream and turquoise completed a charming room.

'Anything you want you have only to ask for. Rita Clarke, my cleaning lady, will be in tomorrow at nine. I shall be out.'

Sheena could not suppress a nervous laugh which turned into an uncontrollable giggle as he was speaking. Her legs were still unsteady and her heart was beating far too fast from her struggle with Ross and the inner battle she had waged with herself. But her sense of humour burst through, although tinged with bitterness.

Ross was not amused. Leaning indolently against the door frame he said curtly, 'What's the joke?'

Sheena shook her head, wiping tears of mirth from her eyes in childlike fashion with a finger.

'I was just thinking,' she answered huskily. 'I suppose this is what a mistress feels when her lord and master shows her to the flat he has bought for her.'

His dark eyes were sardonic. 'Splendid training for your future would you not agree?'

Sheena was equal to his mockery. He looked so confident, arrogant and virile that she longed to throw something at him.

'When you have finished insulting me perhaps you will show me the bathroom,' she said with dignity.

He gestured to a door in the far corner of the room. 'Through that door,' he said.

Later, back in Dawn's apartment, Sheena undressed and glanced at herself in the long wall mirror. This was how Ross Carlyle had expected to see her if he had enticed her to share his bed. Her body was satin smooth with slender lines, firm breasts and gently curving hips. She quivered on recalling the practised eyes Ross ran over her, mentally undressing her. It was rotten luck for him to appear on her horizon so near to her leaving London. But she had to accept his challenge. It would not have given her the peace of mind she wanted if she ignored it. Bemused as she was by her own feelings concerning him, Sheena did care what he thought about her. After she had put him right on that score, Ross Carlyle would be erased from her mind forever.

What she would never forget was the power he had to summon up the most primeval emotions in her while remaining unmoved himself. But what else did she expect from a man who was an expert on women? She felt a shamed kind of anger that he could ignite a wave of passion, giving her a shocking desire to press herself close to him, to feel the comforting warmth of his hard body against her own. No other man had ever affected her in this way. He had routed her confidence and her peace of mind, and she had to restore it before she left his service. At least Dawn had got away, which reminded her that her sister would have to be told about her new job. There was no reason to give details. Time enough to tell Dawn when it was all over.

She wrote to Dawn the next day saying that she had a temporary job that provided her with somewhere to live. She would keep an eye on the apartment, so there was nothing for Dawn to worry about. Her one wish was for Dawn to be happy.

When Sheena met Rita Clarke, after Ross had collected her and her belongings, she was immediately at her ease. She was about forty years of age, married with two sons at university. She was energetic, slim and smart, and her dark neatly-combed hair was not yet grey. Her smile was wide and friendly and her welcome was meant sincerely.

Rita made no secret of her admiration for Ross. 'He deserves the best every time,' she told Sheena. 'He makes me wish that I was twenty years younger.'

Sheena spent the day getting used to the lay-out of the place. She made morning coffee for Rita and learned a few things about Ross. Until recently he had not entertained more than four people. They were mostly business associates, intelligent and well mannered. He had his quota of girlfriends, but he never seemed to single any out for a long term relationship. 'The man can cook too, which is something to his credit,' Rita went on. 'He must be a marvellous business man also because he is going to work in the States next year.'

Sheena swallowed unable to explain why she felt so down.

'What is his business exactly?' she asked.

'He takes over once-successful firms that have gone into liquidation and makes them successful again. He is also very good at persuading investors to put their money in the companies concerned.'

'Good for him,' Sheena murmured without enthusiasm, and moved restlessly after finishing her coffee. All this hanging about was getting her down. What was he playing at anyway?

For two days Sheena did not see her employer. The office staff were not due back until the following Monday and the place seemed like a morgue when Rita had gone. Sheena had gone through her cookery books and selected menus which could be served at the drop of a hat and meals of several courses. The deep freeze had been checked and the addresses written down of suppliers in case they ran short of essential fresh foods. She had wild ideas of going out for the day to see more of London for there was much she hadn't seen as yet, but she was too honest to go out in her employer's time since he had already paid for her services. There had been no mention of time off, but on the third evening when Ross had not shown up she dressed for going out.

At seven o'clock when he had still not shown up or contacted her Sheena put on a boldly striped taupe and blue cotton shirt with a sailor collar with a matching culotte-style skirt. Then draping a black velvet jacket around her shoulders she trod into high heeled sandals, picked up her handbag and went out. It was easy to pick up a taxi at the corner of the road from those cruising by, but as she put out her hand Sheena realised that she had not made up her mind where to go.

The long car which stopped for her was not a taxi.

'Going somewhere?' Ross drawled opening the car door.

'No . . . I mean . . . yes . . .'

'Hop in quickly,' he cut in impatiently. 'Come on.'

He glanced briefly at her slender figure, at the blue of the dress deepening the violet of her eyes.

'I'm sorry,' she began on an apologetic note. 'You never said when you would be back, so I decided to go out. This is the first time.'

'Got a date?' he asked, steering the car out of the traffic to speed ahead.

'No.'

'But you have somewhere in mind?' he persisted.

Sheena said the first place that came into her head that she had not been to.

'The Beefeater.'

He raised a dark brow. 'The one in St Katherine's Dock by the Tower of London,' he said politely.

'That's right.'

He frowned. 'So be it,' he murmured.

Sheena stiffened. 'You don't have to take me. I was hailing a taxi when you appeared.'

She glared at him, her violet eyes sparkling mutinously. He was wearing a very smart suit in grey flannel with a cream shirt and neat tie. He had evidently been out on business and was on his way back to his apartment.

'I can come back with you to the apartment if you want a meal,' she said. 'Actually I had no fixed place to go. You must be looking forward to having a shower and putting your feet up.'

He tossed her a sardonic glance then gave his attention to the road.

'The Beefeater doesn't exactly call for a change of clothes. Have you been there before?' he asked drily.

She shook her head. 'No, I haven't. I just thought it would be rather fun.'

'On your own?'

'I believe it's quite lively, with sing-songs and that.'

'It's lively enough,' he said laconically, adding no further comment.

Glancing at him beneath her lashes, Sheena felt the impact of his masculine charm with mixed feelings and a flush warmed her cheeks. His profile, strong and handsome, revealed no emotion. She swallowed on a dry throat and watched the lights springing up for the evening's entertainment. Taxis swarmed around them like flies, but Ross kept his cool even when hedged in by over-eager drivers.

She clenched her hands in her lap with the feeling that this evening, like the others she had spent with him, was hardly going to be a success. Still, with the revelry that went on at the Beefeater perhaps the evening would not prove to be so traumatic after all.

CHAPTER SEVEN

FOR Sheena that evening at the Beefeater was one to be long remembered. Advertised as an old-English night out they were met at the entrance by wenches dressed in the period costumes of Henry the Eighth, with mob caps and dirndls. They were then issued tickets allocating them to tables with names like Newgate or the Tower of London. The cost of the ticket covered a five course medieval feast with unlimited wine and beer to drink during the meal and entertainment. It was all laid on in the vaults in a long, low brick room.

A group of minstrels sang old folk songs as they entered and Ross steered her away from the honey cake and flagons of mead to the bar. The people pouring in were mostly tourists, a cosmopolitan crowd all set to enjoy themselves. By eight-thirty everyone was seated at their table and given a scroll printed in prose style at which Ross chuckled with wry amusement.

'Ye Gods,' he murmured. 'Shades of Sweeney Todd. What will they think of next?'

He grinned at Sheena seated next to him and her heart tilted. The two wenches allocated to each table gave him almost their undivided attention, and she did not blame them for he was easily the most madly attractive man in the room. Jugs of wine and beer were filled and refilled and guests passed plates to dole out their own portions from cauldrons.

The master of ceremonies, the Beefeater, dressed in traditional style announced the arrival of the King and Queen with their courtiers made up of the guests who volunteered to join them. The Beefeater sang with a trio and bade everyone join in. Then the mock Queen sang *Plaisir d'Amour* and the first course of the meal was announced. There was a ten minute interval between each course for lively entertainment and it was an uproarous evening.

It could have been the respite they both needed. Ross joined in the festivities with gusto although Sheena knew that it was hardly his idea of an evening out with a girlfriend. He had a pleasant baritone voice and before the evening was half way through they were laughing at all the absurdities. Their immediate companions at the table were French and as Ross could speak their language fluently they got along famously.

As he was driving her back to the apartment, Sheena's head began to nod and she jerked herself awake when she found the side of her face against his shoulder. She cast him a surreptitious glance wondering how long the friendliness between them would last. Inwardly sighing she fell to wondering what it would be like to be married to him. During the evening she had only caught a glimpse of what he would be to someone he loved. He was no boy. He had been around a long time and he had not let her see much beyond his charming façade. Despising her as he did, he was even less likely to lower the barriers between them. Like herself he seemed disinclined to talk and most of the journey was made in silence. They were nearing their destination when she thought that some thanks on her part were called for.

'Thanks for taking me out this evening,' she told him huskily. 'It was certainly an experience.'

He glanced at her and said, 'You could say that a good time was had by all. Did you enjoy it?'

'Yes, I did. To begin with it was nothing like I expected. What about you?'

Again he gave her a swift glance and he smiled. 'I think we sang very well together and it's obvious that you can enjoy yourself without being rowdy,' he said mildly.

Sheena clenched her hands together in her lap. His remarks had relegated her to the peasant class. Maybe he thought that was her idea of entertainment, that she had chosen The Beefeater because it was in her class. After all she was his employee. She made a mental note of the menu: Paté, fresh leek soup, smoked mackerel, a portion of chicken, vegetables and Anne Boleyn's apple flan. Perhaps she could serve it up one evening to his guests. But of course she would not. Suddenly she felt terribly tired and dispirited. Sheena closed her eyes and did not open them again until he drew up at the apartment.

He used his key to open the door and flung it wide for her to precede him inside. For a long moment he stared down at her aura of auburn hair, the wide eyes the colour of drenched violets in a face pale and somehow defeated.

'You need your bed and I know I need mine.' Then his hand was on her back urging her forward. 'Good night. Sweet dreams with no thoughts of Sweeney Todd to scare you,' he said firmly.

Sheena could not be sure he had kissed the top of her hair on passing him, but up in her room she leaned back against her closed door with tears in her eyes. What had she expected for goodness' sake? After all, he was only her employer. She tried to remind herself of that while she prepared for bed. She was on the verge of sleep when it dawned on her that Ross was the kind of man she could love, the only man she could ever love enough to want to spend the rest of her life with. Working for him with this shattering knowledge was not going to be easy. She would have to fight frantically and coldly any tender or vulnerable feelings where her love for him was concerned. She loved him and he despised her.

Sheena put aside her oven mitts and breathed a sigh of relief. Everything was under control and the dinner she was preparing was in the final stages of preparation. In the dining-area the table had been set for eight people and she had set a match to the pile of apple logs on the raised hearth of the fireplace. The dining-table was immaculately set, with a centrepiece of red and white carnations, the glassware sparkled and the silver gave off a rich gleam to enhance the well laid-out table. With a satisfied sigh she returned to the kitchen knowing that it could pass a military inspection. Her habit of washing each pan after it had been used meant less harrassment when washing up after a number of people. All that needed to be done later was to put the used dishes in the dishwasher.

A glance at the kitchen clock told her that she had time to wash and change before the guests began to arrive. Her dress was a Butte knit in eau de nil with a camisole top of inserted lace. The picot edge of the skirt was full and swirled around her slender legs setting off the simple elegant line of the dress. The only hint of colour was in the turquoise ear-rings and necklace. In high heeled sandals, she looked feminine and sophisticated. Her reflection in the mirror gave her confidence and the knowledge that her culinary offerings that evening could not be excelled, Sheena returned to the kitchen to don her overall and set about the last stages of preparing the meal.

'Is everything all right?' enquired Ross lazily leaning against the door frame behind her. 'If you will tell me what wines you want I'll get them.'

Regaining her wits Sheena slammed the oven door

and swung round to see him looking devilishly attractive in evening dress.

She said sweetly, avoiding his gaze, 'Everything is taken care of. The wine is on ice and I shall be ready to serve the meal when you are ready.'

He took his time looking her over from her flushed face and luminous violet eyes down to the pretty high heeled sandals and delicate ankles.

'You aren't planning on keeping that overall on all evening, are you?' he queried on an uplifted brow.

Sheena was saved an answer by the sound of the door bell chimes. The first of the guests had arrived, and Ross went to let them in. The hot hostess trolley was filled at last and everything was ready when Sheena shed her white overall.

The doorbell had pealed several times and all the guests were there with a drink when Sheena walked in. A quick survey told her that there were two middle-aged couples and three men. But it was the one behind Ross as everyone turned to look at her who demanded attention.

'Dinner is ready when you are,' she began when Ross strode to her with a martini.

'Have a drink first,' Ross said handing her the glass and drawing her forward. 'Sheena, this is Peter and Mavis Kent, George and Carol Flint, Bill Waters, Farley More and Ted McBride.' His white smile included them all. 'Sheena is acting as my hostess during a short sojourn in London.'

They all greeted her politely, but Ted McBride came forward with a delighted smile on his face.

'Sheena I've been wanting to contact you, but no one knew where you had gone.' A wiry man of medium height with thick grey hair and alert grey eyes, he came forward to greet her. 'I hope you are still out of a job because I want you to come back. We are starting up again with Ross here to help us out.

Sheena stared at all their faces realizing that she was meeting the directors from her former employer's business group.

He turned to Ross who was watching them narrow eyed. 'I hope I have prior claim on the best secretary I ever had,' he said. 'Trust you to find her.'

'So you two know each other,' Ross said mildly. 'Shall we sit down at the table? We can talk later.'

They all made a move towards the dining-area and Sheena put down her glass and went to the kitchen. Ross had allowed his eyes to linger on her before moving away. The look was one of reserved politeness. Ted McBride's association with her must have come as a surprise, but he had not turned a hair. It was as if the man who had taken her out the previous evening had never existed.

The dinner was a huge success with everything being eaten with obvious enjoyment.

'I see you haven't lost your magic touch where cooking is concerned,' Ted McBride remarked when Sheena wheeled the hostess trolley around the table for everyone to have a second helping of her apple crumble. He was sitting next to Ross. 'Sheena is one person you won't have to put right if she comes back to join the firm, Ross. She was certainly an asset to the company. You didn't say anything about her, you dark horse.'

Sheena was now standing behind Ross who refused a second helping of the delectable dish. She saw the neat row of clipped dark curls at the back of his strong neck above the immaculate collar and she longed to put out her hand to touch their springy softness. One strong brown hand was curved around his wine glass, the strong lean fingers curled loosely showing the neat, well-shaped nails.

Before he could answer, she said jerkily, 'Ross . . . Mr

Carlyle didn't know I had worked for you, Mr McBride.'

Ted turned to look at her in surprise. 'But surely he saw the reference I gave you?'

'No . . . I . . . that is . . .' she broke off as Ross cut in curtly,

'Sheena's sister is a friend of mine. I knew Sheena personally before I engaged her.'

Ted grinned, 'Do I scent a romance between you and Dawn? She's a pretty woman, but not a patch on Sheena.'

Ross said sardonically, 'Let's say we are good friends.'

Ross had made the coffee and wheeled out the used dishes which Sheena placed in the dishwasher. In the living-room he had replenished the logs on the open fire and now he was handing out cigars and cigarettes. The guests, replete from a marvellous meal, were now enjoying their coffee and liqueurs and Ross made Sheena join them.

Ross, coffee in hand, stood against the fireplace looking down upon his guests. They were grouped neatly on the array of sofas by the fireplace.

'So, Sheena worked for you, Ted? For how long?' he queried and drank his coffee.

'Oh, let me see.' Ted looked thoughtful as Sheena replenished his cup. 'Quite a while. She left for quite a long time after working for me for a fairly long time, then she came back . . .'

'You mean she didn't work?' Ross insisted.

'Not for two years.'

Ross said jocularly, 'Didn't you pay her enough?'

'Oh yes. She was with her sister, Dawn. She . . .'

By now Sheena had gone pale. It had taken all her skill to refill coffee cups as they were handed to her without spilling half of it.

She said hurriedly, 'I'm sure you didn't all come here this evening to discuss my past. Am I to understand that Mr Carlyle is interested in setting up the firm again?'

Ted grinned. 'I have hopes now of getting back again, thanks to Ross here. Everything is in the early stages yet, but I think that things are moving in the right direction.' He gave her an appraising look.

The soft bloom of colour in her cheeks heightened the violet of her eyes. Her hair was an aura of red and her smile resting on one of her favourite men was very sweet. She had moved around gracefully, filling coffee cups, her slender pearl tipped hands fluttering nervously when she came to Ross to avoid his touch.

Ted went on, 'You certainly look well, Sheena. I always knew that you would blossom out if given the chance.' He turned to Ross who was still leaning nonchalantly against the fireplace. 'Here is one of our greatest assets, and I want her back. I know that Sheena would come back if given the chance.'

Ross waved the suggestion airily away. 'One thing at a time. We have to cover a lot of ground first. That company you were mentioning . . .'

Sheena went to the kitchen to make more coffee, wishing that the evening would come to an end. The meal might have been a great success, but the event had still been an ordeal. At least the company present had been agreeable. There had been a lot of laughter, mostly stemming from the witty remarks of Ross. There had been times, though, when Ross had appeared to remain aloof as though assessing the qualities of the people present.

He had the knack of putting his finger on the trouble spot of an argument with an occasional comment which would show the other side of the matter in hand. He did not ramble on like some men who loved the sound of their own voice. His opinions were brief and concise, and one could see that he did not suffer fools gladly. His quickness at seeing the flaws in someone's logic, his caustic comments about the rogues in certain businesses, his dry sense of humour, all these things set him above the average business man. He could use his charm at will, but it was not the silver tongued type, rather it was on the arrogant side when he knew that he was right.

Sheena was seeing a side to him that she had never known had existed. She could see now why he had never taken a wife. He loved to work and he did not need any 'little woman' behind him, like many men in his position did. He kept his lovelife separate and he had only to crook a finger to have practically any woman who took his fancy.

So thought Sheena who was making what she hoped was the last pot of coffee. It had been quite a shock to meet up with her former employer again. Much as she had enjoyed working for him, Sheena knew that it would be impossible for her to go back now that Ross was involved. She had to get away from Ross when her present job was over. He was already too dominating a factor in her life and he did not care one jot for her.

Sheena did not dare to analyse her own feelings for Ross. It would be foolish to do so. It would be better to try to put him from her thoughts whenever they were together and more important to do so when they were apart.

Ted McBride was the last guest to take his leave and he took Sheena's hand on parting.

'When can you dine with me?' he asked her eagerly, ignoring a frown from Ross. 'Mereal and the kids will be chuffed to hear that we shall be seeing you in the near future.'

Ross broke in curtly, 'You are jumping your fences

too soon, Ted,' he growled. 'Possession is nine tenths of the law.'

Sheena's irritation was plain in her voice though she met his dark eyes steadily.

'Let us get this straight, Mr Carlyle. You employ me. You don't own me,' she told him firmly. 'If I want to dine with anyone who asks me, I will.'

There was an awkward silence while Ross looked at her probingly. Then Ted spoke.

'I'll telephone you, Sheena,' he said looking at both Ross's and her unyielding expressions.

'Good night, Ted,' Ross put in coolly. He draped an arm around Sheena's shoulders deliberately so that Ted would notice it.

Ted lifted a brow. 'I must hand it to you, Ross. You have certainly brought out a very different Sheena Denton from the one I used to know. She is lovely. I don't blame you wanting to hang on to her. If you can do as much for McBride's I will be eternally grateful,' he said drily. 'Good night to you both.' He had gone before Sheena could say a word.

She turned on Ross in fury. 'Of all the nerve,' she berated him heatedly. 'Of all the arrogant, swollen-headed types I have met, you beat the lot. How dare you say that you possess me? You certainly don't, and furthermore you will not dictate as to who I see in my own time. Understand?' Shaking his arm from around her shoulders, she placed her hands on her slender hips and glared at him mutinously.

Unperturbed he took her arm in a firm hand and returned her to one of the cosy sofas by the log fire.

'Calm down,' he said mildly as his dark eyes roved over her slender, shaking figure. 'There's nothing to be gained by losing your temper.'

As soon as she had flopped down angrily on to a sofa, Sheena saw that it was a mistake. Towering over her, he seemed more menacing, reminding her that they were alone together in his apartment and that she was at his mercy. While he might be scrupulous in his business dealings, he could be unscupulous with his women. The man had to have a flaw somewhere.

'Say what you have to say,' she said grimly. 'I am tired, so make it short.'

'First of all,' he began slipping off his jacket and tossing it on to the back of a chair. 'What is McBride to you? Did you chicken out when his company went under, in a hunt for bigger game?'

She looked up at the wide shoulders filling the tailored silk shirt, the well-cut lines of his face seemed as if carved in mahogany in the muted lights, and lowered her gaze swiftly on reaching his mouth. She could never look on his lips without a longing to feel them on her own. If he thought she was going to be goaded into a slanging match that would end with the usual result of his grip turning to caresses, he was mistaken.

'Sure I did,' she cried defiantly, suppressing her desire to hit him. This was ridiculous. It was essential for her to keep cool. A clear head was needed when she was dealing with Ross. With a deliberate effort of will she added. 'Are you going to help him?'

'It's part of my job and it's a wonderfully rewarding one. Which I am sure yours must be, only in a different category,' he murmured insultingly.

Warily Sheena rose to her feet, finding him much too near, but he did not step back. Pulling away slightly, she smiled up at him.

'Since you know all about me, there is no point in us talking any longer,' she said brightly.

'Not everything,' he corrected her his eyes on her mouth. 'There is much, much more I would like to know.'

The intimation was not lost on her and again she heard a faint warning bell within her mind. It had not occurred to her until now that she was leaving herself wide open to his insults in harbouring his wrong impression of her.

'I'm tired,' she told him candidly, avoiding his dark eyes. There was a gleam in them which set her heart thudding with a mixture of fear and longing. She really was tired and not up to fighting him. What a situation. 'I'd like to go to bed.'

'Now that is where I am solely in agreement with you. But I don't suppose you meant with company?'

He had put out his hands and was drawing her closer. She quivered wondering what he would say if she said yes.

'You know that I meant,' she said stiffening. 'And if this is all the thanks I get for all the effort I have put in for a successful evening, then you are more of a swine than I thought you were.'

He gave a wry smile. 'You are wrong,' he said softly. 'I am so indebted to you for your help this evening that I wanted to give you a hug and a kiss. There's nothing wrong in that surely?'

'No?' she whispered, disturbed by his nearness and the scent of sandalwood soap that hung about him. Better give in to him over one kiss than to fight him and rouse other basic emotions.

Hen had deftly taken off his tie with one hand and opened the buttons of his shirt. Then he was pulling her close to the warmness of his chest until his thighs pressed hard against her as he bent his head. Before she realised it he had slipped the slender straps of the camisole top of her dress down her arms to reveal the briefest of lace evening bras beneath her dress.

The satin sheen of her skin seemed to take him aback. He shook his head sadly.

'What a hard heart is doing beating in such an exquisite body I'll never know,' he groaned. 'I wonder if I am wasting my time in trying to make you into a different person from the scheming siren you appear to be.'

The feel of his firm lips on her own sent a delicious shiver of anticipation along her spine and she was lost. That first kiss seemed to go on for ever and she never wanted it to stop. At first contact it was like an electric shock going through her from top to toe. Then the gentleness that parted the sweet softness of her lips deepened with an almost cruel urgency too strong to resist, even if she had tried to. Her arms went around his body, loving the lean warmth of it, until she ached for the passion he had leashed against her.

His lips moved down at last to the tender hollow in her throat and down further to the gentle swell of her breast and when she quivered, he kissed her roughly on her tremulous mouth with an increasing desire. He seemed to possess her completely, his mouth draining her lips of their sweetness while his hands moved down over her back to press her against him. Her soft curves seemed to have melted into the warmth of his body with her every nerve responding to the virility in him. In the physical and emotional tumult he was arousing in her, Sheena felt too blissfully happy to even to attempt to resist him. It was only when he reached for the hook of her bra fastening that Sheena came to.

'Please Ross. Let me go,' she breathed, willing herself to draw away from his demanding mouth.

He let her go, slowly looking down into her face as if she was some mathematical problem which disturbed him greatly.

'At least there is fire beneath that calculating exterior,' he murmured. 'You are a mixture of contradictions.'

'You've said that before. What did you expect?' she asked wishing that he would remove his hands altogether from around her. Her resistance against him was nil and there was a cold feeling around her shoulders where his arms had been. Her need of him, the yearning for his kisses, was like a drug and she closed her eyes against the passion still smouldering in his.

It was inevitable that he should take her lips again as they quivered with need. Threading his fingers through her luxurious hair he had her head firmly between his hands as he moved his mouth tantalizingly over hers. Gradually his hands slipped down to her waist and hers crept around his neck. Their bodies became one column and Ross unleashed some of the passion at her response. Sheena returned his kisses with an equally ardent passion until she suddenly realised what the outcome would be.

He released her at the pressure of her hands against his wide chest. She could not look at him, so embarrassed was she at her own response to his lovemaking. She just dashed away silently to her room.

Sheena was still trembling when she undressed for bed. What was there about him that made mincemeat of her emotions? Never before had she allowed anything to undermine her will as Ross did when he kissed her. At least he had not let her down on getting to know him better. He was infinitely nicer and a man of integrity where business was concerned. While she could trust him, Sheena knew that she could not trust herself where he was concerned. She slipped into bed knowing that he was in the same building as herself and it was small wonder that she had a restless night.

The next day was a normal one. It was as if the night before had been a dream. She made her bed, put on a pair of baggy shorts in primrose and a white sleeveless top and went up to breakfast. Ross had apparently already eaten and gone out. He had left the things he had used on the working top in the kitchen. Sheena helped herself to orange juice, made some toast and boiled an egg. The day lay before her empty and useless. Why on earth couldn't Ross leave some instructions as to when he would be back?

She put the used dishes with those that Ross had left thinking that Rita would not like the idea of finding the dishes washed when she arrived. She had nothing to do so there seemed no reason why she should not go to Dawn's apartment in case she had written. On her arrival there, however, she found that there was no post. When she left the flat a large car was parked at the kerbside—it could only belong to Ross. He sat there, obviously waiting for her.

'Hello there,' he said with a smile. 'How would you like a day out on the Thames?'

She slipped into the seat beside him. 'How did you know that I was here?' she asked evading his question. While the prospect of spending a day in his company was heaven, Sheena wondered if it was wise.

'I didn't,' he confessed giving her slender figure in the Aztec shorts a look of appraisal. 'You were out when I returned to the apartment and this was the first place I tried, I'd only just arrived when you came out of the flat.'

She glanced at his dark lean face and the strong hands on the car wheel. Already her heart was beating double-time at his nearness.

She said warily, 'Have we been invited on someone's boat?'

He had set the car off at speed. 'No, the boat is mine. It's quite a nice size. We are calling back to the apartment where Rita is putting up a picnic basket. While we are there you can collect your swim suit. The weather forecast is good so we can make the best of it. Next week I shall be too busy to have this kind of time off.'

That day on the Thames with Ross was sheer heaven to Sheena. She had put on a bikini beneath her shorts and stood beside him as they skimmed across the water. She threw back her head to let the wind rush through her hair giving her a wonderful sense of freedom. They were alone in a world of their own and she cast him a glance, thankful that her eyes were concealed beneath the sunglasses.

Ross wore no sunglasses and he was stripped to his shorts. Neither sun nor wind appeared to bother him and his mahogany skin was like satin. The biceps of his arms were powerful and firm and his muscular forearms were sprinkled with dark hairs. Her glance slid down his torso to the firm hands piloting the boat. They looked immensely strong and competent as he gripped the wheel and he seemed disinclined to talk.

Ross pulled in to a woodland glade at the side of the river and carried the picnic basket to a shady spot beneath the trees. He laid out a rug for Sheena and opened the picnic basket. To Sheena the food and wine were nectar from the gods. They ate with enjoyment then lay replete to sleep the meal off.

Sheena was awakened by someone pushing a strand of hair back from her face and her eyes flew open to find Ross lying beside her supporting himself on one elbow as he caressed her face.

'Is it time to go?' she asked still only half awake.

'Not if you don't want to,' he murmured. 'Do you?'

The faint fragrance of his aftershave and the touch of his hand on her face brought back the weakness she always felt in her limbs, when he was near. Part of her wanted very much to stay while the sensible instinct was to get up and run before it was too late.

He saw the indecision in her violet eyes and rubbed a thumb meditatively along her jaw.

'Don't you want me to give you a good time?' he asked softly, dangerously. 'What's wrong with a kiss or two?'

'Nothing,' she admitted. 'But you aren't playing fair are you?'

He frowned. 'Of course I am. We are both free and over twenty-one.'

'That isn't what I mean and you know it.'

He shook his head and her hand was drawn to caress his strong brown throat.

'Do you deny that you brought me out for the day in order that I wouldn't be in when Ted McBride telephoned?' she insisted.

He grinned, but the teasing glint in his eyes faded, to be replaced by a look that set her heart pounding. His fingers tightened on her chin and he captured her eyes.

'I didn't like the way he looked at you. The man is half in love with you and being married won't prevent him from dating you,' he growled.

Sheena laughed. 'But that is absurd. I've known the man for years, and . . .'

He was unconvinced. 'He wants you back,' he finished for her, moving a strand of hair from across her eyes. 'For more than one reason.'

'That's ridiculous,' she protested, lowering her eyes away from his probing. 'Besides, didn't you say that I had run away from him because he wasn't wealthy?'

'He could be in time, though. I have a very influential friend who could set him up and when his work load is streamlined he could very well pick up quite quickly. Most of the firms I've taken charge of have been over staffed and underworked. McBride's is no exception.'

His hands were cupping her face and a wave of

gratitude for what he was going to do for McBride's washed over her. Her fingers were kneading his powerful shoulders and tears glistened in her eyes.

'Thanks for wanting to help Ted,' she said huskily.

It was an invitation that Ross could not overlook. His mouth descended on hers and his arms went around her drawing her ever closer. When her arms crept around his neck his kisses became more demanding, but instead of drawing back, Sheena opened to his passion. Sliding his hand in between the top of her shorts and her loose top he caressed her back. Soon she was massaging the muscles of his back with the same urgency. Her passion soared with his and she was deaf to the sound of people approaching the river bank in their boat.

It was Ross who eased off. 'You would think we would have some privacy here, wouldn't you?' he whispered against her lips.

'It is probably no one we know,' she whispered softly, her hands sliding reluctantly from his shoulders. 'They must have seen your boat.'

'Yes, probably the same idea in mind as I had, and like Barkiss the lady is willing.'

Sheena was shaking with laughter. His arms tightened around her.

'Do I take it that the lady in question has your approval?' he murmured.

Her breath caught in her throat as his dark eyes bored into her and his gaze lingered on her mouth rosy from his kisses. Her fingers thrust themselves through the thick dark hair and her lips trembled.

'I suppose . . . she has yours,' she replied cleverly.

'You are avoiding the question,' he said hoarsely and she closed her eyes against the desire in his, drawing his head down, urging his lips on hers.

His kiss was bruising, but suddenly he lifted his head. 'Come on. We are going back to the boat. You go to my head like too much wine and I never over indulge.'

Something flickered in his dark eyes and disappeared before Sheena could put a name to it. Whatever it was, it acted as a warning to her common sense. It was incomprehensible the way he got under her guard. She was in no danger from him—it was her own idiot emotions which carried her away. There was the rest of the day to get through so she had to be on her toes.

Back on the boat she had undressed to her bikini and was stretched out on deck in the sun. His eyes slipped appreciatively over her pretty figure as he gave her an iced drink, but he made no comment. Sheena knew that he had not missed an inch of her delectable body and she quivered inwardly as their fingers touched. She almost spilled her drink in an effort not to touch his hand and she was rewarded with a mocking glance.

Drat the man, she thought furiously. He knows how vulnerable I am to him.

They were back in his apartment by early evening. He had a telephone call to make and he was going out later.

Sheena went to her room with a sense of let down. The whole evening lay before her, she would be alone and without anything to do. It didn't help to know that Ross had planned it that way to keep her from Ted McBride's invitations out. Perhaps Ted had left a message with Rita and with this thought in mind she went upstairs to the kitchen.

Rita had left her a note to say that Ted McBride had called her several times and had left his telephone number. She rang him immediately. He was delighted to hear that she would go out with him that evening and he arranged to pick her up at seven-thirty.

Sheena had used the telephone in the living-room to

call Ted and as she put it down her eyes raised to find Ross leaning with negligent ease against the door frame.

'Not losing much time, are you?' he said quietly.

Her violet eyes flashed angrily. 'And what is that supposed to mean?' she cried, quivering at the shock of his unexpected appearance.

There was a disturbingly intent quality in his eyes as they caught and held hers and it deepened that trembling inside her.

He said coolly, 'I am doing business with McBride's and I don't want you coming in at this juncture. I'd rather you didn't see him this evening. I never mix business with pleasure and you are doing just that by going out with him this evening.'

Sheena stiffened her erect little spine and looked at him chillingly.

'The McBrides are old friends of mine and it has nothing at all to do with you,' she retorted.

'I've told you that man is more than half in love with you. You are encouraging him by going out with him this evening. I suppose you are well aware of your own charms. Married men of middle age go for young slender saplings like you, but you don't need me to tell you that. You have your eye on the main chance. Why don't you go for some younger, single man who can give you far more than anyone like McBride?'

Her eyes flashed blue fire. 'You, for instance?'

He held up a hand theatrically as though warding her off.

'God forbid,' he said roughly. Then his tone softened as he looked at her. 'I like you, even though I don't respect you. And I hate to see you making a mess of your life. Think it over. After this evening you are going to be busy entertaining.'

CHAPTER EIGHT

SHEENA was trembling upon reaching her room over what Ross had said. He did not respect her. She clenched her hands in mortification. Who did he think he was? She would show him. All her gratitude to him for what he was doing for McBride's was gone. He must have thought it a worthwhile investment or he wouldn't give it a second thought.

She said the same to Ted McBride that evening as they sipped their aperitif in the dining-room of a select hotel. He still could not believe that there was a way out for him, and he had told her so.

'Ross told me this evening that he is going to be busy in the immediate future, entertaining, so I don't think he is wasting much time in getting down to business. He has the right people interested but, of course, it has nothing to do with me,' she reassured him.

'I know that. All the same I think you have brought me luck,' he said reaching across the table to take the hand resting there.

Sheena looked down at the large hand covering her smaller one and smiled embarrassedly.

'I'm glad I've brought somebody luck,' she said. 'But I don't see how I could. But I do wish you well, Mr McBride. I always will.'

He squeezed her hand. 'It's Ted, Sheena. Do you know,' he said softly, meaningly, 'I think that you and I could do great things together?'

'I'm sure we could, Ted,' she answered relieved that the arrival of the waiter made it necessary for him to remove his hold on her trapped hand. Sheena had always respected Ted McBride and she was sure that he had never stepped out of line like having an affair back home. But it seemed that Ted McBride away from his wife was a very different proposition and this was what Ross had been warning her about.

The meal was delicious in every way but Sheena felt that she was eating sawdust. It was a shattering thing to see one's ideals being crushed in the dust of life. She fell to thinking about Dawn and Frank and she hoped with all her heart that he would not let her sister down.

One thing she was definite about and that was that she was going home alone in a taxi to Ross's apartment. She had seen the light and was fed up in more ways than one. Ted had very reluctantly agreed after she had refused to go with him to his room after the meal. There was a light on in Ross's apartment when she arrived back at around nine-thirty and she went straight to her room. No doubt he had been out to a date and brought the woman back with him, she thought bitterly.

It was too early for her to go to bed. In any case she was feeling too restless. Wearily she shed her clothes and after relaxing in a warm perfumed bath she put on a robe and curled up on her bed with a paperback book. She had lost herself in the story when the door opened and Ross stood there.

'So you are back. What was it, short and sweet? Or did you call too late and he had another engagement to fit in with yours?' he growled leaning against the closed door.

Sheena had been frightened out of her wits by his untimely entrance. 'Ross!' she croaked heart pounding until it was deafening to her ears. 'How dare you burst your way in here without knocking? Get out!'

He had shed his jacket and his shirt was open half way down to show his wide powerful chest. His thick dark hair was rough as if he had run his fingers through it and his eyes looked almost black. His gaze ran over her in the dressing gown opened at the neck to show the gentle swell of her breast.

'That's a nice body you have there,' he said softly coming slowly towards the bed after taking one lunge from the door. 'Suppose I finish off what your old friend started?'

The book fell from her nerveless hand and she drew the wrap closer around her.

'You've been drinking,' she accused when he had sat down on the bed beside her.

'I've had a drink,' he admitted. 'I have also been working.'

'Tiring was it?' she asked insolently. Anger was her only weapon against him and she was using it for all she was worth.

'You little . . .' Ross pulled himself back with an effort. 'If you mean what I think you mean that makes two of us,' he growled menacingly. 'Let's console ourselves, shall we, for a disappointing evening?'

He bent over her, then tore open the wrap and set his mouth to her throat and breast. Sheena quivered. It was like coming to the mouth of a furnace and the heat of his passion burned her up. She placed her hands against his chest where his shirt was unbuttoned and pushed, but to no avail. His lips sent her senses whirling and she closed her eyes as the masculine scent of him increased the force of her own desires. Holding her mouth captive with his he slipped a hand inside her wrap sliding it round to caress her waist and hip.

Wide-eyed, Sheena knew that she was helpless against his strength and her own weakness as his mouth covered hers once again in a deep, disturbing kiss which ignited the smouldering fires within her. She could not believe that a date he had made had let him down. Yet he appeared to be punishing her for something that had happened to him. The fierce warmth of his hard body was seeping through to her very bones as he whispered against her lips.

'Let's find out how mercenary you really are,' he said, finding her mouth again in hard, angry, yet dangerously sensual determination.

Sheena's anger reached a white-hot intensity at his insolence and she shut her mouth tight against his assault. But Ross forced it open again with a deft movement of his fingers and thumb. When she tried to utter a protest he smothered it with a mouth which stood no nonsense. Moving it sensuously over her quivering lips, he was telling her in kisses that she had no chance against him. She clung on to her resistance knowing that the moment she lost it, Ross would have his way with her.

Then gradually his kisses became less cruel and his arms less rigid. To Sheena this change of mood in him was more dangerous than his cruelty. Her whole body responded to the magic of his nearness and her arms went around his neck pulling him more tightly against her. It was Ross who pulled away lifting his head and she could feel his breath on her temples when he spoke softly in her ear.

'There, you see, you have all the soft feminine instincts after all. Pity it has to be material gains that will buy them from you,' he murmured his lips moving down from her temple to her mouth.

Sheena jerked her head away. 'Maybe I am stringing you along like you are me,' she said tightly.

'But you like me making love to you,' he whispered. 'You tremble like a captive sparrow. There you are.' He slipped a hand inside her wrap and laid it on her bare flesh above her heart. 'Your heart's thudding away like mad.'

'No, don't . . . No,' she gasped as his touch set her body on fire with emotion. 'Let me go.'

'Your lips tell me one thing and your body tells me another. Which is the true answer, my frightened Sheena?'

He tipped her head back and fastened his mouth on hers again. She stiffened and tried to remain impervious to his demands. His lips were moving gently over hers, not cruel this time, but evocative and teasing. The wrap was slipped from her bare shoulder and his mouth was tracing a trail of kisses down it on to softer flesh. His hands moved around to her back beneath the wrap and one moved up the front to find her breast.

When his mouth sought hers again Sheena was almost sick with longing for him. He was driving her crazy with frustration and a raging longing for him to possess her completely. It was her lips that sought his now and they met in a breath-stopping kiss. Her mouth submitted to his kisses and her body pressed close to his. Time stood still as he lifted her above the earthly sphere into heights she had not known existed. Then as suddenly as he had taken her, he let her go, and she was left staring up at him and dragging her wrap close around her trembling body. Descending from the heights of esctasy in his arms Sheena realised with an appalled shock how close she had come to surrendering to him. The agony of it was, that she loved him with her whole heart. His look of contempt stung her to the quick for she was vulnerable now against his every action. This was how it had to be from now on.

Had she have known what the job would cost her in emotion she would never had taken it in the first place. Dimly she was aware of him speaking.

'You thought that I was going to take you to bed with me, didn't you?' he said scathingly. 'No chance. I was only proving a point to my own satisfaction. I wasn't stringing you along, as you seemed to think. I was searching for the real you beneath that cool surface. Tell me. That time you left McBride's employ did you go to live off your sister?' He lifted a hand disparagingly. 'Don't tell me. I don't want to know. Hell! What do I care what you did?'

Sheena bit hard on a trembling lip. 'Please leave me alone,' she pleaded, her blue eyes bright with tears, her face pale and defeated. 'Just leave me alone.'

He rose from the bed then abruptly, without a backward glance left her room. Once alone she climbed out of the bed and sank down into a chair, stony faced. It would have been easy to tell him the truth about those two years she had spent willing Dawn back to the land of the living by devotedly nursing her. Then she shrugged at the idea. He probably wouldn't believe her. Angry with herself at being so upset, Sheena took on another thread of thought. He was perhaps gradually seducing her until in the end she could succumb to his mastery without any qualms of conscience. What a fool she was to be taken in with him.

Ross was fully occupied with work when his office opened again after the holidays. He had one or two guests for dinner almost every night, but after Sheena had done what was required of her she went to her own room, leaving Ross with his guests talking business. She kept out of his way as much as possible and they fell into the habit of being employer and employee.

When she was not needed at his apartment she went to Dawn's apartment, while she was at Ross's she read, or listened to music. Sometimes she went around the shops and had lunch out. These outings were fraught with tension as she looked around for Ross to appear unexpectedly as he had done in the past, but he did not. Then one morning he was there when she came down to breakfast looking heartbreakingly handsome in cream slacks and coffee coloured shirt.

Hastily she was going to withdraw but he gestured her to sit down, looked at his watch and drained his coffee cup.

'We are going out to dinner this evening and a show,' he said without preamble as he rose to his feet. 'Be ready at seven sharp.'

'Just like that,' Sheena murmured beneath her breath to empty air for he had gone. Inwardly sighing she set about getting her breakfast, wanting to be out when Rita arrived at ten. Somehow she had to learn how to handle him without any emotional encounters. Her heart had been wrenched at the picture he made of virile manhood. His well-cut mouth had relaxed into a smile at her startled look, but the dark eyes which had met her had no particular warmth, just faint, cool regard.

It was not going to be easy to continue working for him under the present atmosphere, but she would not run away. That part of him that was tender and gentle would never be allowed to show itself when she was around. He had no belief in her integrity and still less in her desire to be independant of anyone. The pity of it was that she had no one to whom she could turn. She had to rely on her own judgment every time.

Ted McBride, her former employer, had gone back home with a contract in his pocket which Ross had signed, thus giving his firm a new lease of life. He had promised to get in touch with her and although Sheena had hoped that he wouldn't, she had just nodded and agreed half-heartedly.

She went to Dawn's apartment that day and in the evening dressed with attention to every detail of her appearance, her nerves on edge expecting him to appear before she was ready. She had heard him arrive at the apartment and she was quite prepared for him when he put in an appearance. She met him at the door feeling a warm tide of colour rush to her face when he confronted her in a dark suit and white silk shirt. He gave her the kind of cursory glance that took everything in, the figure-hugging skirt and batwing top in coffee coloured lace effect down to the high slender heels of her strapped sandals showing her delicate ankles and very pretty legs.

Her luxuriant auburn hair was swept back and held with a band of brown velvet ribbon offset by wooden rings in her ears.

He said with some amusement, 'You are a mixture of the pagan and the sophisticated.'

She murmured something, hoping that he would be in a more amiable mood as the evening wore on. After he had seated her in the car, he drove off without speaking, his profile remote as he gave his attention to his driving. Sheena sat with her hands clasping her evening bag tightly, wishing that he would break the silence.

At last she could stand it no longer. 'Is this a business outing?' she queried in a small voice.

He tossed her a brief glance. 'No. Just a night out.'

At their table in the restaurant he ordered an aperitif before their meal and when it had been served leaned back in his chair.

Sheena sipped her drink and looked around at the tables occupied by a select smartly dressed clientele. Then turning back to her own table her eyes collided with his. Again her face flooded with colour and she blurted, 'The show we are going to, what is it?'

He looked bored but he was amiable enough. 'It's supposed to be good.' He smiled wickedly. 'It isn't one of those strip shows or anything that might embarrass you.'

'I didn't expect it would be. I'm surprised that you

are taking me, though, you must have lots of other women to choose from.'

'You are the one I chose. You are easy on the eye. You know how to dress,' he mocked, stripping her with his eyes.

'Am I supposed to feel flattered?' she demanded resenting his insolent gaze.

'You know what?' he leaned forward to speak to her softly. 'I think that you have been so busy watching Dawn that you've lost yourself in her shadow. You are a very attractive woman. Why don't you shed those conniving little plans of yours and concentrate on being what you are—a beautiful, self-sufficient woman?'

'What exactly does that mean? You are my employer, you know.'

He shrugged wide shoulders. 'See what I am up against? Don't you realise that I find pleasure in your company?'

'I thought I had been engaged to entertain your guests,' she replied icily.

'I'm giving you a break. You won't always be here.'

The waiter came and put an end to their conversation for a while. It was true what he said that she would not always be there. The thought instead of uplifting her, however, only served to make her feel worse. The prospect of getting to know him better might have intrigued her before she had realised her love for him. As it was, he had to remain an enigmatic, infuriating man or she could finish ending up being emotionally scarred by the experience.

The show was a very entertaining comedy and Sheena laughed her way through it her laughter a descant to Ross's deeper chuckle.

'Not bad, was it?' he said, as he seated her in the car to drive back to his apartment.

Sheena shone up at him. 'I enjoyed it. Did you?'

'Yes. Not a bad night out so far.'

She shot him a brief sharp glance. Now what did he mean by that? she thought warily. Forewarned was fore-armed, she told herself grimly.

'Come in for a night cap before going to your room. I don't know about you, but I never could go right to bed after an evening out.'

They were her sentiments exactly, but all the same Sheena paused, unwilling to prolong the evening yet aching to do so. Reluctantly she let him lead her to the living-room of his apartment, suffering his light hold on her elbow. After seeing her seated on one of the comfortable sofas by the fireplace, he shed his jacket and turned on the stereo for some music.

'Would you like a nightcap?' he asked with a raised brow walking with an easy grace to the drinks cabinet.

'No thanks.'

He turned. 'Would you care to dance?'

'Dance?' she echoed.

He pulled her to her feet and took her into his arms. The music was low and soothing, a slow number, and they moved in perfect harmony. Sheena almost had her head on his chest when his hand moved slowly over her back in a deliberate caress. It was obvious to her that he was intent upon getting some response from her. If only he knew how much response he actually aroused in her treacherous body. She longed to draw him closer, to shut her eyes and feel the warmth of his arms around her, but while his hold was comforting his face remained expressionless.

She marvelled that her whole being could be trembling with extraordinary feelings and urges, yet he could remain cool, calm and collected. Sheena was of average height, neither too tall nor too petite, but he towered way above her.

Ross was looking down on the lovely sheen of her

auburn hair thinking involuntarily how very attractive she was, a grave-faced girl as pliant and fresh as a young willow. Until now his affairs had provided him with a sensuous delight, all the more enjoyable because they had been fleeting. Now he was discovering that there was something about this girl, whom he had reason to dislike, a disturbing vibrant something which while it intrigued him also filled him with a desire for her. Without realising it his hand closed on her waist almost savagely and he held her with a vice-like grip against him.

Startled Sheena looked up. Meeting the dark intent look, she was shaken out of her dream world to harsh reality. She went rigid with tension and abruptly he released her.

'Would you like some coffee?' he asked politely.

He did not wait for a reply but, strode to the kitchen to make it. Sheena sank down on to the sofa, knowing by the look in his eyes that it was better for her to accept the offer. All she could think about was the sudden cruel grip on her waist and her quick upwards glance encountering the unreadable expression in his eyes. Had it been anger or dislike, resentment or lust? Whatever it was, it had set her heart thundering painfully against her chest.

He came in with the coffee and handed her a cup. Then he sat down near to her on the sofa. She drank her coffee without looking at him. Was it her imagination that she felt his antagonism as something tangible?

'We appear to have run out of conversation,' he said, slowly sipping his coffee.

Sheena put down her empty cup. 'I am rather tired,' she confessed, striving for a lightness in her voice. It was a terrible effort to pretend to be light-hearted when an enveloping misery settled upon her. 'I think I'll turn in.'

Her heart thudded with deep painful beats as he rose from his chair to reach for her hands and pull her out of her chair into the circle of his arms. The contact with his hard body sent shivers of extraordinary emotions through her. She was determined not to give in to him. With her arms tight at her sides she let him take her lips and taste their sweetness. Then she pushed him away.

Walking to the door with a dignity that sat well on her slender shoulders, she turned to address him, her hand on the door knob.

'Goodnight, Ross. Thanks for the evening out. I enjoyed it.'

Without her noticing, he had moved across to her in a few strides, slamming the door closed and towering over her menacingly.

'The evening isn't over yet by any means,' he whispered, slipping his hands beneath her hair and cupping her face.

His kiss was almost her undoing. It seemed to take her very soul from her body, but she stuck to her determination not to give in to him. When he lifted his head to look down at her face, the hardness in him strengthened her resolve to keep her cool.

'Never give up do you?' she said huskily.

He raised a dark brow insolently. 'Does that mean that you have?' he whispered.

She quivered at the look in his eyes which patently had nothing to do with love.

'No it doesn't, and now I'd like to go to bed . . . alone, if you don't mind.'

It was torture to keep the quiver out of her voice for his nearness sent ripples of excitement through her. His eyes narrowed.

'I wonder if you would have given the same answer had I not made it clear that I wanted no serious involvement . . . marriage? Am I too big a risk for you to take?' he jeered.

'I work for you, remember?' she reminded him bitterly.

He hauled her back into his arms and kissed her then, his mouth deliberately bruising and uncaring on her quivering mouth. Emotions ran through her like flames, burning her up. Sheena closed her eyes and willed herself to remain passive in his arms. Then gradually he drew away to gaze down on her pale, controlled face. Her violet eyes were a luminous glow, the only colour to enhance the burnished auburn of her hair. Something gleamed for a moment in his dark eyes then it had gone before Sheena could even begin to analyse it.

'I could change your mind, but I think a night cap would do more for me tonight.' He almost pushed her away. 'Go and get your beauty sleep by all means. Perhaps it would be wiser if you were to stick to your cooking. Good night. Sweet dreams.'

Upon reaching her rooms she did not breathe freely for several moments. It had been a close thing and Sheena knew that he was as aware of it as she was. Her fingers touched lips still throbbing from the punishment of his. She felt weak and tremulous, but was filled with relief that she had escaped so lightly. At least she had held her own against him, but it was small consolation when every bone, nerve and sinew in her body cried out for him.

After that she was wary of accepting invitations from him. Fortunately he entertained a lot and she became adept at avoiding being alone with him before they retired to their rooms. Without consciously realising it, she discovered that they were two of a kind in their likes and dislikes. They both liked sailing and motoring in the country for picnics. They liked the same kind of music and neither of them were great talkers. The lapses of silence between them were enjoyed.

Gradually she began to know him better and in doing so found herself relaxing more in his company. It was only in the evenings after dinner that she had to be wary of him. One evening they had both been out with a small party of his friends to a new nightclub where Sheena had thoroughly enjoyed herself. The entertainment had been first class and she was still smiling when Ross drove them back to the apartment.

He had gone with her to her room door and she had looked up at him, lips parted, eyes dancing, at the memory of the very funny act she had seen at the nightclub. But her smile became strained when their eyes locked and she felt his hands gripping her shoulders. His kiss was not seductive. It was passionate and brutal. Sheena suffered it without a quiver and when he lifted his head his voice was curt.

'You asked for that,' he said tightly.

Anger rose inside her. She hated him for spoiling what had been a very enjoyable evening. He had the kind of friends who, like himself, were intelligent, nice people.

'Why? Because I looked happy?' she cried scornfully. 'You can't bear to see me happy can you? I really enjoyed this evening and you had to spoil it.'

'Spoil it with a few kisses? Thank your lucky stars that kisses are all I'm taking,' he said. Then his lips were again cruelly pressed against her quivering mouth. Her head was forced back over his arm as his lips ravished her. He appeared to have lost all control as his passion was unleashed and Sheena was shattered. When his hands began to explore the curves of her body and his mouth moved down to her neck, she strained against him.

'Stop it,' she cried in the few seconds that her lips were free. 'Let me go.'

'You don't want me to let you go and you know it. You have been asking for this all evening,' he growled. 'Don't you realise that there is provocation in everything that you do? That sweet husky laugh you have, the way your eyes shine with the tears of mirth in them, the way they darken when you look at me as you try so valiantly to read my thoughts. There's a poetry in you that drives a man wild.'

Sheena went rigid while her every nerve quivered at his nearness. 'In other words I turn you on,' she scoffed. 'You are only turned on when you want to be, but you aren't going to do anything at my expense.'

His eyes narrowed cruelly. 'That is just what I am going to do. I am going to make love to you until you beg me for more.'

'Never,' she cried, squirming wildly in his arms.

He had scooped her up and carried her swiftly through the half-opened door of her room to throw her on to the bed. Then before she realised what was happening he had shed his jacket and he was lying on the bed beside her. All reality vanished as his lips parted hers and made tender demands which were more lethal than his brutal kisses. The length of his body against her, the sweetness of his kisses were a seduction combined to overcome all her resistance. The zip fastening of her evening top was down before she noticed and with one swift movement it was down over the arms he had pinioned by her sides.

Then his lips explored her soft skin, the hollow in her throat, the shadowy niche between her breasts while his hand roamed softly over the curve of her hips. He had her arms fastened by his other arm which coiled tightly around her. Sheena was gasping with roused emotions as his mouth came down on her own in a long, dizzying kiss—she was unaware when he released the fastening of her bra.

But she did feel his hand cupping the soft swell of her breast before moving down towards the soft plane of her stomach.

'Ross, you've got to stop,' she cried on breath regained as he lifted his head. 'You know what you said about being committed? Well you are committing yourself. Don't you see?'

He said nothing, but just stared at her pleading face.

'Suppose I want to commit myself? What then?' he demanded.

Sheena shook her head desperately. 'You don't. You just want to hurt me because I am everything that you despise.' Tears drowned her eyes, but she went on valiantly. 'Hate me, but don't end up hating yourself.'

For long tight seconds he just stared at her, his dark eyes narrowed, his fine nostrils dilated. Then he rolled off the bed and in one fluid movement was on his feet.

'Damn you,' he said on a low growl and left the room.

CHAPTER NINE

For a long time after Ross had left her, Sheena sought for the sense of elation her victory had achieved. Instead it was something of a let down. To her dismay she found herself wanting him under any conditions. She loved him wholly and completely. She was sure of it with a deep sickening knowledge that frightened her. She was going to hate it when she had to leave and go back home. If she had needed any proof that he did not love her in return it was there in the way he could move away from her and leave her as he had done. She went to sleep on a pillow that was wet with tears.

There was no sign of Ross having had breakfast the next morning when she went into the kitchen around eight o'clock. Mechanically Sheena made toast and boiled an egg. She had lain awake in the early hours of the morning, the victim of fitful sleep, teetering against leaving right away or giving him notice. Yet she knew that on seeing him, she would do neither. There was no sign of movement anywhere and she set about eating with little or no appetite. She managed two fingers of toast and was pouring out a second cup of coffee when there was a movement behind her. Her heart beating alarmingly told her that it was Ross and she plucked up the courage she had been seeking.

'I'm leaving today, Ross. There are outside caterers you can contact until you get a replacement. I can't take any more. I've had enough.'

Her voice was perfectly steady, but her hands holding the coffee percolator were shaking so much that she had to put it down.

'I haven't,' he said strolling round the table to haul out a chair on which he sat straddled legged over the seat with his arms across the back facing her. 'You know as well as I do that we can't say goodbye. Things have gone too far for that.'

Sheena glanced up at him then lowered her eyes again. He looked strong and vital, his dark hair still damp from a recent shower, the wide shoulders filling the white cotton shirt open at the strong brown throat. He looked tanned, fit and uncaring and there was a gleam in his eyes that brought the hot colour to her cheeks.

'I'll qualify that,' she told him huskily looking down at her half filled coffee cup. 'Things have gone too far for us to do anything else but say goodbye.'

'I'm going to marry you,' he said firmly.

Sheena's expression registered shock and incredulity. 'What did you say?' she croaked on a dry throat.

'I said I am going to marry you.'

'That's what you think,' she scoffed and rose in her chair not liking the look in his eyes. 'A girl likes to be asked not told and even if you were to ask, in your case the answer would be, no.'

He was up in one sinuous movement and he was filling the kitchen area with a challenging, dangerous maleness.

'Come here, Sheena,' he said softly, dangerously. She quivered at the note of underlying passion in his voice.

'There is nothing more to say,' she blurted, conscious of her heart thumping madly at the excitement he was generating.

Why was it that he could upset her with just a look or a gesture? He rose away from the chair he had straddled and she stepped back realising that he was quite serious.

'Neither of us is deaf,' she said with a hint of hauteur. 'We don't have to go into a clinch to discuss perfectly logical things.'

But the expression in his eyes was anything but logical. He really meant what he said, and common sense told her to respect his seriousness.

'What man is logical when he is aching to kiss his future bride?' he said with a wicked gleam in his eyes. 'I'm going to kiss you until you agree to marry me, and that isn't all. We are getting married as soon as possible, in case I change my mind.'

'Really,' she cried scornfully. 'Who do you think you are giving me orders like that? No. No way would I want any more to do with you than I do now. I can't wait to get away from you.'

She took a step back at the expression in his eyes. There had been no emotion at all in his voice when he had spoken of marriage, and she had a strong desire to weep. Not long ago her thoughts were running along the lines that she would have him at any cost. Then common sense told her that a marriage based on pure physical need plus a business partnership which made her valuable to him in more ways than one, said that she was better away from him.

'You are a liar, Sheena,' he said softly advancing towards her purposefully. 'I have only to take you in my arms and you can't help yourself. Why did you accept my offer of a job if you didn't like me?'

'What girl who was unemployed would turn down such a good offer of a roof over her head and a very pleasant job?'

'That's all it was?' he questioned ironically.

She said calmly, 'It could help me a lot when I look for a new job.'

He walked slowly towards her and this time Sheena did not move. Although she was literally at his mercy she had no intention of letting him know that she was more afraid of her own emotions than of him.

'I want you to look me in the face and tell me that

you aren't interested in me as a man, that you don't care for me at all and that you never could.' he said placing a finger under her chin and forcing up her face.

She quivered at the cold brilliance of his dark eyes, the grim set of his well cut lips. There was no love in him only a determination to have his own way. Divorce would be easy enough for a man in his position when he had tired of a hastily taken wife.

'I'm not infatuated with you like you are with me,' she answered truthfully longing to add that she loved him. She said, 'You want to reform me and you speak as an employer, not a lover.'

The hard line of his mouth softened tilting into a half smile.

'So, I should have been more of the lover first? Is that it?'

His mouth touched hers while his hand slid around to the nape of her neck to hold her head firmly. Then her body was being moulded against him and the old magic began to work. His lips were gentle and teasing at first until he felt her response. Then the kiss deepened and she could feel the passion in him being slowly unleashed until they seemed to be fused together in one pulsating column. Her arms slid around his neck and she gave him the sweetness of her lips not flinching when his kisses became more demanding.The demands of his mouth drowned all coherent thought as she clung to him.

Desperately she tried to keep her mind alert to fight the unwanted flow of passion invading her whole being as his tongue parted her lips and his hand moved to caress her soft curves. Sheena wanted this moment of passionate fulfilment to go on forever while Ross took something from her that she could never have back.

Presently he began to chuckle with sheer mastery. 'You couldn't kiss me like that,' he whispered half teasingly, 'if you weren't fond of me. By the way, I have a present for you. It's in appreciation of all you have done for me.'

He took a long jeweller's case from his pocket and snapped it open. On a bed of purple velvet lay a delicate cameo on a fine gold chain, and matching ear-rings. He watched her face as she stared at something she had wanted for a long time. She had been looking round for a cameo locket such as this, but never in a hundred years could she have bought one as exquisite as this one.

'It's beautiful . . . the strange thing about it is it's something I have wanted for a long time. But Ross, it's too expensive for me to accept,' she admitted honestly.

He stared at her for so long that Sheena felt like screaming. Then it occurred to her that her refusal did not fit in with his image of her. She should have grabbed it with her greedy little hands—that would have been more in character with the sort of woman he thought her to be. Then he took the necklace from the case and put it around her neck, taking out the ear-rings to clip them to her ears.

'You will take them and I go with them,' he said firmly.

The glow in his eyes made her quiver and though only the tips of his fingers as he had put on the jewellery had brushed against her skin, she felt the latent strength of his hands.

'I want neither.' Her hands were already fumbling with the catch of the necklace when his fingers closed in over them like steel.

'Remove it and you can expect reprisals,' he warned. 'I mean what I say.'

Already the warmth of his hands on her was undermining all her resistance. What was wrong with her? Had she no more pride than to let him take possession without any demur? His hands had closed fast over hers and now he was drawing her to him with a gleam of passion in his eyes.

'It isn't as though you really care . . .' she began.

'I want you. That is enough.' Lowering his head his mouth closed over hers and Sheena did not resist.

Her surrender along with his devastating expertise made her ache for unknown delights which she knew he could give her. He had released her hands and they were around his neck pulling him ever tighter against her trembling body. When he moved from her mouth to her face with teasing kisses, her lips sought his.

Just before he came back to it, he said, 'Are you going to marry me?'

Drowned in bliss she could only whisper her acceptance. Her eyes were closed because she could not meet the passion in his without giving her love away. This time his kiss was unrestrained and his arms around her were so tight that she could hardly breathe, but Sheena exalted in the pain as she pressed against him. It was Ross who drew away, albeit reluctantly, and when she opened dazed eyes it was to see the mocking smile on his lips. The sight of it made her move to escape and he let her go.

'By special licence in three days,' he said laconically. 'So you had better be ready.'

Love, Sheena discovered, was a sickness which gnawed at one from within. There was no cure for it, neither was there any respite. Sleeping and waking her thoughts were filled with Ross. There was nothing she could do about it. She was helplessly and hopelessly in love with him.

Sheena did not see Ross for those three traumatic days preceding her wedding. One moment she was aching for him to return, the next she was dreading it. There was no reason why she could not run away and go back home, but she was in love with him too deeply to even think about it. What if they were married for only a short time? She would have the memory of being married to the only man she would ever love.

Apart from him taking her birth certificate and the necessary information she had no idea whether the wedding would take place in a church or a registry office. She bought a beige suit and matching lace hat wishing wistfully that she could have dressed in white and had the wedding in the church back home. It was not that kind of a wedding, though, at least not on his side.

She was awakened at four in the morning on the Saturday by someone kissing her. Sheena opened her eyes to see Ross sitting on the bed, smiling at her wickedly. His kiss had been cool from the early morning air of outdoors and when his lips pressed hers again, she met them eagerly, parting her lips to his arrogant demand and giving the response he silently demanded. Her eyes closed she revelled in the familiar scent of his aftershave, the strength of his arms and the intoxication of his kisses.

'You go to my head like wine,' he murmured against her willing mouth. 'Do you mind if I seduce you now?'

His mouth was moving into her neck and her fingers were threaded through his crisp dark hair. Not one word about loving her, she thought despairingly. But perhaps he would in time, when she had proved not to be the scheming little baggage he thought she was. Her mouth moved hungrily beneath his. Nothing mattered but being with him, belonging to him.

He was the first to pull away. 'On second thoughts we had better wait. If I take you now we shan't be in time for our wedding,' he told her with a wicked grin.

Bemused, she said on breath regained, looking

tousled and very sweet, 'What time are we getting married?'

'Lunch time and a reception at a hotel. Everything has been taken care of. My secretary has seen to it.' He kissed the tip of her nose. 'He is to be best man.'

The wedding went off without a hitch, a simple registry office service with his staff and friends gathering around later to shower them with confetti. As he slipped the ring on her finger Sheena was aware of the grip of his fingers and the fierce strength of his hand, but his kiss at the end was cool and short.

The reception went on until about four in the afternoon with Ross consulting his watch from time to time a little impatiently. Sheena had been moving among the guests with him trying to remind herself that she was no longer his hostess but his wife.

'Let's go,' he said taking her arm and piloting her out to his car.

She went with him marvelling how a simple service had changed everything between them. There was an exciting air which they enjoyed in a companionable silence. The look in his eyes when she had the courage to encounter them brought the hot colour to her cheeks and he seemed to find her touch as moving as she found his. Small gestures, a glance, a smile seemed to be charged with electricity between them.

There was a lot of laughing when he scooped her up into his arms and carried her up to the apartment. Setting her down on her feet he bent his head and took her lips fiercely. Sheena wound her arms around his neck and the world receded. He had carried her into his bedroom and she was aware of the bed behind them. Then she was lost in his embrace.

'We are going out this evening to dinner to celebrate on our own,' he whispered between kisses. 'But we don't have to wait until we return do we?'

She wanted to tell him then that she loved him no matter what he felt about her. 'Darling, I want to tell you . . . that I . . .' she began.

'Stop talking,' he growled and carried her to the bed.

'Please, Ross, let me take off this nice suit,' she begged laughing. 'And I am sure you will be more comfortable without yours!'

'Point taken,' he said, albeit reluctantly, and took off his jacket as the door bell chimed. 'Who the devil can that be? No one knows that we are spending one night here before we take off on our honeymoon.'

Sheena had slipped off her jacket and she went to the wardrobe to find that Rita had transferred her things from the flat below.

She said, 'You don't think it might be someone planning to break in and they are trying the door bell to see if anyone is at home?'

'We can soon sort that one out,' he answered grimly leaving the room.

She had stripped down to her bra and panties when she heard Ross returning and he was not alone. There was a woman with him.

'Sheena?' Dawn shrieked flabbergasted. 'What on earth are you doing here?' Her face as she swung round on Ross was ugly with anger. 'You said you had a surprise for me. I don't find it funny.'

'You haven't heard it yet,' Ross told her unperturbed. 'Sheena and I were married today and we certainly did not expect you to call.'

He was leaning against the door frame nonchalantly eyeing his new bride and liking what he saw. Sheena's face was flushed with surprise and embarrassment, her hair was an auburn cloud around her head and her violet eyes were wide. For several moments she stood there in all her shapely beauty forgetting that she was undressed. The sight of her pretty figure seemed to add fuel to her sister's anger.

'Why you two-timing little cat,' she snarled, her hands clenched tightly in her rage. 'You didn't like Ross Carlyle. Oh, no . . . but you managed to get rid of me while you married him.'

Sheena backed against the bed. 'But you've married Frank. What difference can it make to you if I have married Ross?' she cried in bewilderment.

Dawn placed her hands on her hips in high dudgeon. 'Who is Frank? I've never heard of him?' she spluttered in her fury. 'You know very well I went to the States on a modelling assignment. I never went to marry any Frank and you know it.'

Sheena sat down on the bed to look at her sister as if she had taken leave of her senses.

'Do you mean you didn't marry him?' she said hoarsely.

'There was no one to marry, was there? I gave you a holiday at my expense and this is what I get for it.' Dawn was shaking so much she could hardly speak as she swung once more to Ross. 'You know that I only went to model, Ross. I told you in the letter I left you, that is if my sweet sister gave it to you?'

'She did,' Ross agreed ignoring Sheena and looking intently at Dawn.

Suddenly Dawn was all sweetness and light. 'Then you must know what a little cheat she is. Oh! If only I'd come back a bit sooner. Poor Ross. I'm so sorry for you.'

Ross raised a dark brow and pushed himself away from the door frame to stand up to his full height. 'I think that I can manage to look after my own affairs, Dawn. Now if you don't mind leaving I should like to talk to my wife,' he said quietly.

With a look that was venomous enough to kill, Dawn glanced at her sister then simpered up to where Ross was standing.

'You do believe me, don't you, darling?' she pleaded catching at the lapels of his open shirt.

He looked down at her with no change of expression. 'I believed what you had written in the letter. I saw no reason not to do so.'

She said softly, 'I was hoping to pick up where we left off.' Her hands slipped up his shirt front to rest lightly on his square-set shoulders. 'I don't know how an intelligent man like you could have been taken in by Sheena.'

'I think you had better go, Dawn. I take it that you aren't returning to the States for a while?' he said without expression.

As they talked Sheena hurriedly slipped into jeans and a sleeveless top then picked up her handbag to search in it feverishly.

'Your keys to the apartment, Dawn,' she said in a dead pan voice. 'I still have some clothes there so I shall be calling for them,' she said placing the keys on a low table nearby.

She could not trust herself to actually hand them to her sister without telling her what she thought about her. If something had gone wrong between her and her Frank it was too bad. She only knew that Dawn was throwing something away, something precious that would never come her way again.

Dawn had flounced out with the long arm of Ross around her shoulders and Sheena stared at the closed door wondering what was coming next. Ross would believe what Dawn told him; he had as much admitted it. She lifted shaking hands to her face. Everything she and Ross had been building up between them had gone. Far from assuring him that his opinion of her was wrong, he was going to think much worse things of her now with Dawn's lies ringing in his ears. What chance had she to prove him wrong?

Sheena moved to the dressing-table to pick up one of of his hair brushes and she was taunted by the scent of masculine cologne. The prospect of days, months, years ahead without him, filled her with misery, and she blinked back the tears.

'Why are you dressed like that?' Ross growled striding across the room while unbuttoning his shirt.

She swung round wide-eyed and apprehensive. 'I thought that this could be the parting of the ways,' she said weakly.

He pulled off his shirt and looked at her between narrowed eyes.

'Nothing has changed because Dawn comes in here babbling some tale or other. I knew what you were before, although I have never found you out in a lie. Still, dishonesty goes along with scheming little minds who are out for the main chance.'

He threw the shirt on to the bed. 'Put on a dress. We are going out as planned. I'm taking a shower and then I shall be downstairs in the office until it is time for us to leave.'

Sheena drew herself up and gave him a defiant look. 'But we have to talk,' she insisted, feeling more uneasy then ever.

'We can talk later.'

She hesitated, not caring for the look in his dark eyes.

'You . . . you mean everything is going on as if nothing had happened?' she stammered.

'But something has happened,' he said softly, dangerously. 'We are married and I am going along with that, Mrs Carlyle.'

'But suppose I don't want to go along with it until we've talked over what's happened?'

'I think you will.' He gave her a wicked smile. 'Don't

forget that if you do protest, I shan't know whether you are lying or not, shall I?'

When at long last they were ready to leave Sheena shuddered inwardly as his fingers cupped her elbow in silence. The situation might have heightened it, but to Sheena there was an aura about him of unleashed masculine strength which not even the tailored white silk shirt and dark suit disguised. The width of his shoulders, the powerful chest narrowing down to long muscular legs moving nonchalantly from narrow hips all combined to remind her that the evening was not going to be an easy one.

They were at the door of the hotel when she pulled back.

'Do we have to go through with this?' she pleaded.

With maddening slowness Ross held on to her arm and looked her over from the top of her auburn hair to the high heeled sandals on her feet. It was the kind of glance that took everything in, his gaze lingering on the creamy rise of her breast just visible at the vee neck of her gown, the cinched waist and the gentle curves of her narrow hips.

'We are the same two people who were married this afternoon,' he said coolly, as he guided her firmly into the hotel restaurant.

Sheena was caught in a welter of emotions as they were shown to their table in the luxurious restaurant. What she could not understand were her new husband's motives in going on as if nothing had happened. Of course he would be in an awkward position if they were to part on their wedding night. He would look pretty foolish upon meeting all his friends and business acquaintances under those circumstances. She looked around the restaurant to see it filling up rapidly with a select clientele, then glanced across at Ross to find him studying her expression.

'Is anything wrong, Mrs Carlyle?' he asked, raising one dark eyebrow. 'I hope you don't object to champagne?'

The wine waiter was there, the cork popped, Ross approved the flavour and lifted his glass to hers when the waiter had gone.

'May all our future surprises be pleasant ones,' he said with a mocking inflexion. 'To us.'

Sheena fitted in with his mood. After all, this was her wedding night and they were certainly celebrating it in style. The hollow feeling in her stomach might not have needed food to assuage its aching intensity, but it helped. She lost track of how many glasses of bubbling liquid she drank, but she was quite alert to the curious and predatory expression in her husband's eyes.

Later they danced, but only once. Looking down at her flushed face, he said, 'Let's go home.'

In the car she looked at his formidable handsome profile, and took the plunge. 'Ross, I . . . must tell you . . .' she stopped to search for the right beginning and then despaired of finding it.

He did not turn his head but kept his attention on the road.

'I'm not interested in anything you have to say,' he cut in curtly. 'According to Dawn you were out to get me and you fought all the way to achieve your objective. Fair enough. You got me and I have no argument with you about that because I was out to get you too. I'd say that we deserve each other.'

In the apartment, he guided her to the living-room. 'Take a seat while I make a cup of strong coffee. You certainly celebrated with a lot of champagne,' he said drily.

Sheena sank down on to a comfortable sofa and closed her eyes. Ross thought that she had cheated him, but she would not do so tonight. Although how he could expect things to go on as if Dawn had not come, was beyond her.

He came into the room wearing only his dressing-gown having undressed while the coffee was heating. She quivered at the glimpse of his powerful, hirsute chest visible between the lapels of his wrap, and cringed slightly when after giving her the coffee he sank beside her with his own cup.

'Thanks,' she said. 'I enjoyed the meal.'

He said menacingly, 'I hope you enjoy the rest of the night.'

She said valiantly, 'I shall if you do.'

Her coffee drunk she rose to her feet and made her way upstairs. In the bathroom she cleaned her teeth and picking up her robe found her gown missing. She had quickly snatched up everything she would need in order to be ready before he came upstairs but in her haste had dropped her gown. Opening the bathroom door slowly, she listened for sounds, heard none and dashed into the bedroom completely undressed. Too late for her to retreat, she realised that he was there stooping to pick the flimsy garment from the carpet where she had dropped it.

Like a startled fawn she stood horror-struck, revealing her naked body to his amused gaze.

'Is this what you are after?' he mocked. 'Well, don't just stand there. Come and get it.'

She had a choice of either snatching her nightdress or running back to the bathroom—she realised the latter course would make her look pretty foolish, so she made a lunge, her arm was seized as she stretched out for the garment and she was hauled against him. The flimsy gown was tossed contemptuously aside and his mouth closed on hers. Her senses were in a whirl as his mouth devoured hers with his kisses that gradually changed from assaults of passionate intensity to the brands of possession.

She responded with uninhibited passion, loving his nearness, the hard exciting masculinity of him.

'Here we are, my sweet,' he murmured against her bruised lips. 'We wanted each other and soon we shall be one.'

He lifted her on to the bed and she gave a gasp on feeling his hard body against her soft, tingling flesh. Ross was not gentle, but nor was he cruel. He explored her with a passionate mouth and possessive hands. Sheena had made up her mind to go along with him, but she found herself sharing his passion. The desire to be loved by him, to be part of him overwhelmed her. He was communicating to her now with his body moving with an insatiable urge to make her his. The passion he instilled in her only seemed to increase his own need. She had not expected any gentle teasing on his part, no gradual building up for the final conquest. There had been too much antagonism and the emotions they had experienced between them were too intense for the slow, gentle preliminaries of lovemaking.

His hands slid over her soft skin while his mouth was making her squirm with longing for him. It was only when her need of him was becoming unbearable that the real union began. After that she only knew that he was urging her desire to flame in harmony with his. Whatever he was doing was what she wanted, and she had never experienced anything so exquisite in all her life. When the climax came, they experienced it together. Slowly they descended from the heights locked in each other's arms from a union so perfect that they were loath to let go.

When they did, they came together again in the natural way of belonging, their passion flared into greater heights of ecstasy sending them replete with lovemaking into exhausted sleep.

CHAPTER TEN

SHEENA moved in her sleep and sighed blissfully. Consciousness was slow in coming for her dreams had been heavenly. She did not want to wake, she felt too lethargic and comfortable. Then it suddenly dawned on her that she was naked under the bed clothes and that she was alone. The hollow in the pillow beside her was the only evidence that Ross had been there.

Events of the previous evening came crowding back in her memory, her surrender, the way she had given herself to him willingly and without restraint. She had never realised there was so much passion in her. How could she face him this morning? And what was he going to do about their marriage?

She swallowed on a dry throat, went to the bathroom for a long leisurely shower then dressed in a beige trouser suit with a bright green silk scarf at her throat. She brushed her silky hair letting it fall into natural waves about her face and used little make-up. One thing that Sheena was determined to do was to look fresh and sophisticated and no way like a woman who had spent a night of love with a husband she was not yet sure of. She was going to appear looking cool and untouched and what was more she was sure there was going to be a confrontation between her and Dawn before the day was out.

Ross was in the kitchen. He was wearing mink coloured tailored slacks and a cream shirt open to show his powerful chest. His hair, still damp from his shower, clung in curly tendrils on the nape of his neck.

'Good morning.' The deep voice seemed to touch

her heart and she dropped her gaze, her heart pounding wildly. His dark eyes were filled with mocking amusement. 'Sleep well, Mrs Carlyle?' he said politely.

She managed a smile, but it became strained on her face when he held up his arms. When she made no move he came forward pulling her gently against him until their bodies touched. Then he bent his head. His kiss was warm and sweet. When she did not respond he forced her head backward and kissed her with a savage intensity which bruised her mouth.

'Don't be so damned submissive,' he growled. 'Is it too much to ask for an honest reaction like last night?'

'That's the only language you understand with a woman isn't it? Sex!' she cried scornfully.

He said harshly, 'There was no sex between us last night. It was love in the purest sense. We are leaving for our honeymoon after breakfast, so eat a good meal. You will be more comfortable when travelling.' He seated her at the table. 'There is bacon, eggs, toast and fruit.'

Sheena was not hungry, but she was determined not to let him see that he bothered her enough to have lost her appetite. She ate and drank without sensation while Ross had his breakfast in between reading his morning post.

The food gave her more stamina to face up to him. What hope had they of happiness if they were going away with nothing resolved, Dawn accusing her of lies and the secret contempt Ross held for Sheena still intact?

'Where are we going?' she asked on drinking the last of her coffee.

He put his post away to give her his full attention. 'I told you—on our honeymoon.'

Her colour went slightly. 'Honeymoon?' she echoed.

'Now after . . . after what Dawn said about me? You must be joking.'

He leaned back on the two back legs of his chair and eyed her with a gleam in his dark eyes which brought the sudden hot colour to her cheeks.

'What has Dawn to do with us?' he said coolly. 'We are married and like I told you before I knew you, I was aware that you were no angel.'

Sheena flinched inwardly. 'I have to see Dawn today,' she said obstinately.

He shook his head. 'There'll be no time for that. How do you feel about travelling, seeing the world?'

She frowned, trying to read his mood. 'I haven't travelled much so I wouldn't know,' she admitted.

His eyes narrowed as he looked at the wide violet eyes, the aura of auburn hair, and he smiled, his teeth a bar of whiteness in his tanned face.

'You look as refreshing as a Spring morning,' he teased. 'You haven't even got that married look about you after a hectic night of making love. You appear to thrive on it. I must bear that in mind.' His smile however did not meet his eyes.

'Where are we going?' she asked nervously dabbing her mouth with the table napkin.

'To a tropical island for three weeks at least. You can buy the kind of clothes you will need when we get there.'

Sheena quivered inwardly. Three weeks of love with Ross and after, what then? Her resolve to give herself to Ross with the hope that he would love her in the end seemed utterly ridiculous now that her sister had made her out as someone who was out for what she could get. Ross already thought she was that kind of a person. Now he had what he would regard as further proof from Dawn.

They had flown into the blue on a very pleasant trip

to see the island Ross had chosen, smiling at them out of an azure sea. To Sheena it had seemed so unreal, with Ross taking charge giving her a feeling of being cared for and loved. If only he did love her. Had she not already loved him, close companionship with him would have endeared him to her. He was marvellous to travel with, making everything run smoothly in the way of handling luggage and booked seats. He was good mannered and charming and oblivious of the admiring glances of the women who happened to wait on them.

Sheena could not explain her reluctance to share three weeks with him in the intimacy of married life, feeling as she did. One part of her wanted it desperately while the other dreaded giving away her love for him. The drive to the villa he had rented did not dispel the apprehension she felt. It was still with her when she saw the bedroom they were to share with the canopied double bed. Niko, the young man who was going to look after them was slender and dark eyed with a pleasant toothy grin.

'I believe he is an excellent cook,' Ross murmured in an aside as he showed them round.

Feeling suddenly light-hearted, Sheena whispered, 'If he isn't, I can always take over.'

'Oh no, you won't. We are on our honeymoon and there are much more exciting things you will be doing and believe me cooking won't be among them.'

He had placed a possessive hand around her shoulders and he tightened it ominously as he spoke.

It was dark quite early and they dressed for the dinner that Niko was preparing for them. Ross had gone shopping for champagne and anything else they were in need of, after seeing that his orders had been carried out on the stocking of the kitchen.

Sheena was relieved that she could wash and dress while he was out. He had not offered to kiss her since they had begun on their journey and despite his charming smile on occasions she had felt a coolness in him.

She put on a dress of *crème de menthe* coloured silk with a halter neckline that showed her creamy shoulders to beautiful advantage. It clung to her every curve, emphasising her small waist and narrow hips to open in a slit down one side to show an expanse of a long smooth leg. The large gypsy gold loops in her ears offset the plainness of the dress. Then with a second thought, she put on, instead, the cameo necklace and ear-rings Ross had bought her.

He had returned when she entered the living-room and he was pouring out drinks. His eyes immediately noticed the cameo as they flicked over her in appraisal. Sheena quivered knowing that he had not missed a thing about her and his eyes lingered wickedly on the expanse of leg when she sat down on a comfortable chair near to a picture window which overlooked a panoramic view of the beach and sea beyond. An enormous moon was already rising among fleeting clouds as she stared out into the darkness.

'Beautifully isolated here, isn't it?' Ross murmured handing her a drink of champagne and deliberately brushing his firm fingers against hers. Then, mockingly aware of her tension, he added, 'Are you scared?'

'Not if you aren't,' she answered lifting her glass. 'Cheers.'

He looked devastatingly handsome in a white dinner-jacket over dark slacks and she lowered her eyes against his intent look as he sipped his drink then put it down on a low table near her. He had not sat down, and he was still looking down at her when he drew a tiny box from his pocket.

'Let's say that this is a belated engagement present,' he said casually, and flicked the box open. 'Like it?'

She was dazzled by the sparkle of the solitaire diamond, winking at her mockingly from its gold setting.

'It's beautiful,' she gasped.

'So you like it,' he said pushing it on the finger adorned by her wedding ring.

Sheena smiled up at him and nodded her heart going like a sledge hammer. 'I didn't expect one.'

'Then the pleasure should be all the greater. Who knows, there might be other things you don't expect?'

His hands were gripping her bare shoulders and she felt his vitality seeping through to her very bones. There was only one thing to do and she raised her head to kiss him on his brown cheek. But his grip on her tightened, hurting her ribs and squeezing the air from her lungs as he swooped down to part her mouth in a long, endless kiss.

Niko came in, and Ross released her as the young man announced that the meal was ready.

Ross took her arm and murmured, 'He's probably been waiting for the past few minutes for an opportune moment to interrupt us.'

'Perhaps he thinks that we ought to have warned him,' she said huskily above the frenzied beating of her heart.

'Never mind,' he growled on a low key. 'After all we are on our honeymoon, Mrs Carlyle.'

And I am not likely to forget it, she thought, as he sat her at the table. The food was beautifully prepared and served with Niko hardly making his presence felt. Ross did nothing to make his presence felt either, but Sheena was aware of him through every fibre of her being.

'Quite a bit of nightlife in the town,' he told her as they ate. 'We'll go in one night for dinner and perhaps to a dance. That is if you aren't too tired with other pursuits.'

He gave her a wicked glance from his dark eyes, but Sheena refused to be drawn as she tried to understand his sudden changes of mood. That brutal kiss just now was meant to hurt. She was sure of that. And that intent look she collided with from time to time did nothing to calm her already taut nerves.

She was glad when he told Niko to serve coffee on the veranda. It was a warm night, but the air was fresher than being indoors and invigorating enough to help her to keep a clear head.

Ross leaned back in the white wicker chair with his long legs stretched out in front of him. In the muted light his features looked sculptured in bronze as he enjoyed his cheroot. Sheena had discovered that he enjoyed most things in moderation, which probably accounted for his splendid physique. She quivered inwardly remembering the feel of his hard, fit body against her soft curves on their wedding night.

Sheena shared the silence which to her was fraught with an almost electric tension. The night was still quite young as they sat drinking their coffee at the end of a delicious meal which she had hardly tasted.

'What would you like to do this evening?' he queried leaning forward to put out his cheroot in an ash tray on the low table. 'Would you like an early night or would you prefer a run in the car?'

Sheena put down her coffee cup. 'Oh! A car run please,' she said in desperation. At least they would be able to talk. She was not at all sure of the expression in his eyes, but she did not intend to dwell upon it in case she lost what bit of self-confidence she had. There was something frightening about the power he wielded over her emotions.

He took the coast road to town and it was heaven letting the cool night air whip through her auburn hair as tendrils caressed her warm cheeks.

Ross said conversationally as he drove leisurely along. 'I didn't see anyone I knew when I came to town this morning for the provisions, but I did notice a select little place where we could stop for a drink and dance if you care to.'

Sheena agreed feeling rather like Cinderella with her joy extended to a three week long honeymoon instead of the final stroke of midnight.

'You are as light as a piece of thistledown,' he said taking her into his arms after guiding her on the dance-floor.

'Thank you,' she replied, moving in perfect harmony with him in the muted coloured lights.

She was glad he had seen no one that he knew and it was only natural to feel rather elated, because she was dancing with one of the most attractive men in the room. They danced several times before returning to a little table and the waiting bottle of wine which Ross had ordered.

For the first time that day, Sheena was beginning to unwind and she found herself meeting his intent gaze more often. They were just settling into their seats at the table, when someone spoke to Ross.

'Hello, Ross. Long time no see?' scoffed a deep cynical voice and Sheena looked at its owner.

He was a very attractive man of medium height with a tight cap of fair curls, and was slender and agile. His light blue eyes moved with open appreciation over Sheena.

Apart from lifting an eyebrow, Ross gave nothing away.

'Hello, Steve,' he said cordially. 'Sheena, this is Steve Fellows. Steve, my wife Sheena.'

'Lovely,' Steve said musingly, holding forth his hand. His handshake and his expression left little doubt that he found her eminently worth his attention and Sheena withdrew her hand knowing that he probably looked at every attractive woman in the same way.

'What are you doing in this part of the world?' Ross asked as he drew another chair up to their table.

'Kicking around. Do you mind if I join you?'

'We are going soon,' Ross said coolly. 'But join us by all means.'

Steve settled himself in his chair, summoned a waiter and ordered a drink for himself after Ross had shaken his head in refusal of an offer of the same.

'The fact is,' Steve began when the waiter had brought his drink, 'I'm married, but I've got a right little bitch.'

'Hard luck,' murmured Ross leaning back in his chair to survey him with narrowed eyes.

'I'll say. She is as mercenary as they come.' He tossed down most of his drink. 'Even told me that she had married me for my money. She is good in bed, but that is the only thing I can say that she happily gives me in return.'

Ross gave a wry smile. 'Then make the most of it,' he said drily.

Ross succeeded in bringing Sheena's eyes to meet his as he spoke and the expression in his made her quiver. She had the feeling that he meant her to hear what he said.

'The way I see it, Steve, you have two options open to you. You either enjoy what she has to give until you tire of her, or you can spin some yarn about your money running out and see how she takes it. She might surprise you.'

They were on their way back to the villa when Sheena said, 'Your friend didn't strike me as a very good husband. I would say that he still has an eye for the ladies in spite of being married.'

He tossed her a surprised glance. 'You would be

right. Steve had too much of everything too soon, a doting mother and limitless money from boyhood onwards.'

When they reached the villa the whole setting was bathed in moonlight spraying the sea with silver. 'It's beautiful, isn't it?' she breathed getting out of the car and looking across the still shimmering water.

He came behind her and she could feel his hard shoulder behind her. 'What about going for a swim?' he said.

'Shall we?' She shone up at him, wanting to put off the time when they retired to bed for as long as she could.

She ran into the villa for her swimsuit and was out again before Ross appeared. The water washed over her limbs like silk and she struck out, swimming under the waves for a while before surfacing.

'How dare you come in without me?' he growled as he surfaced beside her. 'I wondered where you were. You must have been in and out of the house while I put the car away.'

'So what?' He was much too near and she panicked. 'Race you back,' she cried and ploughed through the water as if the very devils of hell were in pursuit of her.

She had a good start before he caught up with her and as she spurted ahead she could see his teeth flash in a wicked grin. He was deliberately letting her go on ahead and she knew it. She would show him. Her breath was hurting as she put everything she had into reaching the beach first and Sheena did not even know whether she had made it.

It was only when she dropped down exhausted that she was aware of him already lounging on the sand waiting for her. Her breathing laboured, she lay back and closed her eyes. She was spent, except for the leaping of her heart as he bent over her.

'Are you all right?' he asked sweeping back her hair and looking concerned.

She took several very deep breaths trying to control the wild leaping of her heart, and opened her eyes. In the moonlight his face was a dark mask, the angles sharpened by shadows.

'Yes. I'm all right. I should have known better, shouldn't I?' she managed on breath regained.

'Yes,' he answered.

She was well aware of powerful shoulders like polished bronze and a firm well-cut mouth drawing her eyes like a magnet. The moonlight made the night almost as light as day and she closed her eyes as his mouth descended upon her quivering lips. His damp body was clamped against hers, his mouth moved sensuously over her and his hand moved down to her thigh. Their lovemaking was accompanied by the rhythmic whisper of the sea, the sand and the warm breeze, but there was little gentleness in Ross.

They made love until the tide came in to wash around them in a hissing rush of surf and sand. Then he scooped her up into his arms and carried her indoors.

Gradually, over the next few days a new sensuality came to her, something undreamed of in her nature. She had taken Ross's advice and shopped for tropical clothes in the town. She bought lovely cotton and silk skirts, dresses and shirts that clung sensuously to her curves and her skin began to bloom like a ripening peach.

Ross appeared to be as keyed up for her touch as she was for his and while she knew that his desire for her was purely physical she was content and grateful that he should want her at all after what he thought about her.

They spent long hours lazing on the beach after

swimming in the blue water. There were leisurely strolls along the crisp golden sand walking together, their arms entwined. They explored the coral reefs and went swimming by moonlight. Sheena loved the night bathing when there were uninhibited frolics in the water and out. Held fast in his arms the world was right and she was safe. It was during these most intimate moments that they learned so much about each other. Most of their likes and dislikes dovetailed, giving her the hope that Ross would change his mind about her . . . perhaps even begin to love her.

Strange that in that three weeks there had been no heart to heart talks between them. The chemical reaction of their sexual attraction to each other flared into life whenever they were alone. In bed his hand pushed through the silky auburn hair to hold her head still while he took her lips with all the ferocity of a man in dire need. He kissed the pulsing hollow in her throat, muzzled in the scented warmth of her shoulder then came back to her lips with a possessive fervour. And Sheena would give him all her sweetness, hoping that one day she would win his love.

The end came with cataclysmic suddenness. They were having breakfast in bed which Niko had brought in to them.

'Our last day,' Ross said taking the cover off his hot breakfast. 'This time next week I will be in the States.'

Sheena picked up her orange juice with trembling fingers. She had forgotten about him going to the States. Did he intend taking her with him? She had to lead up to the subject gradually and she sought for the right approach.

'Ross, do you still regard me as someone out for their own ends?' she faltered trying to keep the tenseness from her voice. 'I mean . . . after what Dawn said about . . . about . . .'

'About you lying?' he helped her out, but was non-committal.

She nodded. 'You know she was overwrought about something? I ought to have seen her before we left.'

'I fail to see what you hoped to achieve,' he said coolly proceeding to eat his breakfast.

Sheena reached for a slice of toast having lost her appetite. Her heart felt cold in her breast.

'What have you and I really achieved?' she said flatly.

'Depends on which way you look at it. We have had a very enjoyable honeymoon. Saying that it all began as a business proposition, our honeymoon has been quite unique.'

'Has it meant anything to you?' she persisted reaching for the coffee to wash down a piece of toast before it stuck in her throat.

'What do you want me to say?' he answered coolly. 'Eat your breakfast.'

She wanted to scream at him. To ask him if he loved her. Instead, she said, 'Are you taking me with you to the States?'

He took down some of his coffee. 'You ask too many questions so early in the morning. Come on eat a good breakfast, there's a good girl.'

Somehow Sheena got through the day finding Ross changeable and puzzling. The result was that she closed up when she really ought to have told him what was in her mind and heart.

They went to town in the morning for Ross to attend to the business of sending off letters and making telephone calls. Sheena bought one or two presents then sat in the car waiting for him. Presently he came towards the car with long purposeful strides.

'You'd better drive back to the villa without me,' he said bending down to look in on her urgently. 'There is a storm coming up and I have to wait for a telephone call. Take care, won't you?'

Sheena started the car, aware that the sky was changing rapidly from clear blue fading into a menacing copper mist. In the distance the sea looked like a pulsing black mass and the air through the open car window was ominously still. She shot the car forward while day turned into night, the heavens closing in around her. The rain did not come until she reached the villa. Even so she was drenched as she made the short sprint to the door.

Indoors she stripped and changed into jeans and a blouson shirt. Niko brought her tea and she drank it, staring into the storm through the window, watching the trees threshing and listening to the shrieking of the wind. It occurred to her, while she watched, that Ross could have gone already out of her life. When Ross had not returned at lunchtime she told Niko to hold it back until he arrived. The storm still raged matching the building tension inside her. She wanted to cover her ears with her hands, close her eyes and grit her teeth and give full vent to her feelings.

Niko said sympathetically, 'I will give you a drink of our local brew to send you to sleep for a while until the storm is over. It is quite harmless and most beneficial.'

Sheena looked wildly at the rain lashed windows and nodded assent. Anything to give her oblivion for a time.

She fell asleep in a chair by the window, a deep, dreamless sleep from which she awakened refreshed. The storm had gone. All was quiet in the villa. Pushing a heavy wave of silky hair from her forehead, she called Niko. No answer. Then, she called Ross. Again there was no reply. She went to the window to see the sun out in full force drying up the garden. Her watch said four o'clock and the storm appeared to have been over for some time.

In that moment of intense silence Sheena had never felt more alone. Niko's absence could easily be explained, for he usually went out for things he wanted, on his moped. But where was Ross? Surely he should have been back by now unless . . . She had been right. He had gone. Her stomach began to churn. She felt sick. What had he said to Steve? Take what she can give until you are tired of her . . . Ross had looked right at her as he had said it. Tormented by her thoughts, she paced the room clenching her hands then pushing a fist against her mouth to help suppress the rising sobs. The next moment she was rushing out of the villa through drenched grass and along quagmire paths to the beach. There she flung herself down on her stomach and beat the damp sand in her agony. She beat it until she stilled, exhausted, wishing that it was Ross she was beating. Damn him. Damn all men.

It was a long time after when with mud-caked feet and damp body, she dragged herself back to the villa to find it still silent and empty of anyone. Going wearily to the bathroom she stripped down to her panties and bra, washed away the sand and mud, then straightened to reach for the towel. She stared in blank amazement at the damp clothes, a shirt and a pair of trousers draped over the bathroom stool.

The next moment she was dashing back into the bathroom with only her panties and bra on. 'Ross!' she cried on seeing him lying on the bed on his back in only his shorts.

He raised his head then his powerful tanned shoulders to grin at her. 'Coming to join me?' he said looking tantalizingly at her delectable figure in a state of undress.

So he had not left her. All that anguish, all that

torment had been for nothing. It was all too much for Sheena. The next moment she was leaping on top of him on the bed pushing him on to his back and pummelling his bare chest with her fists.

'I hate you, Ross Carlyle. Hate you! Do you hear?' she cried in her fury, and the tears ran down her face.

'Eh! Now steady on. What's this all about?'

Sheena was not even listening. She was venting her previously tautly leashed feelings on him, now giving them full rein. Gripping her wrists he swung her over on to her back and hovered above her, pinning her arms above her head.

'Now then. Let's calm down shall we and talk about it?' he murmured, his face close to hers.

He was kissing her tear-wet cheeks, then her mouth and gradually her weeping ceased. By the time he had mopped up the tears she managed to look at him between drenched lashes.

'I . . . I thought . . . you had gone . . . and left me,' she mumbled on a dry sob. 'I know you despise me. You . . . you believed everything that Dawn said about me.'

He frowned. 'Oh, no, I didn't. I had already had a long talk with Ted McBride about you and he told me how you had nursed Dawn through a serious illness and then paid for her training as a model. So when Dawn trotted out her lies about going to the States just to model clothes, I tried a bit of bluff. When I walked her downstairs that day she came to see us I told her that I was going to the States to work soon and it was just possible that I might meet her friends there, meaning this Frank person she was involved with. She broke down then and confessed that she had gone out to marry him, but had changed her mind.'

'Oh, dear,' sighed Sheena. 'I wonder what went wrong. I really ought to have seen her before we left.'

He kissed her trembling lips. 'Stop it. I'd like to bet that she is already on her way back to the States.'

She said, 'She came back because of you.'

'Maybe she did but there was never anything between us to even suggest that I was more than a friend.'

'You could say the same about you and me. Our marriage was only a business arrangement,' she whispered huskily moving her face sideways away from his lips.

'The hell it was.' He released her wrists.

She glared at him as he forced her face round with a firm hold of her chin, and the tears came again.

'Then why have you been so . . . so rough with me . . . and so moody?' she said tearfully.

'Because I wanted you to tell me what I had to drag from Ted McBride and Dawn. Besides I resented you for coming into my life and turning all my plans cock-eyed. I wanted you from the moment you glared at me with those lovely eyes. I wanted to hurt you and make love to you until you screamed for mercy.'

'Ross!' she cried indignantly thrilling to the look of need in his eyes. 'I . . .'

Whatever she had intended to say was smothered on her lips as he took them fiercely. Her arms were around his neck and his heart was striking into hers. She felt his hands move down to her waist crushing her against him. She felt the familiar shock of his hard body turning hers into a kind of burning frenzy and her hands moved over the powerful muscles of his back.

When at last Ross lifted his head his lips curved in a smile.

'I love you, Mrs Carlyle,' he said huskily. 'I'll make it up to you for doubting you, for the rest of our lives. I knew there was something special about you, but it took a honeymoon to show just how special and precious you are.'

Wide-eyed and palpitating Sheena shone up at him. 'I love you, Ross, more than life itself,' she said with a throaty catch to her voice. 'I always will.'

She caressed his dark face tenderly and he kissed her hands.

'You had better,' he growled darkly. 'I am never going to let you go.'

'That makes two of us,' she answered with a look of infinite joy. Her mouth parted beneath his in utter surrender and he drew her to him in fierce possession.

APRIL 86 HARDBACK TITLES

ROMANCE

An Elusive Mistress	*Lindsay Armstrong*	2516	0 263 11069 9
Abode of Princes	*Jayne Bauling*	2517	0 263 11070 2
The Tempestuous Wooing	*Katrina Britt*	2518	0 263 11071 0
A Thousand Ways of Loving	*Joyce Dingwell*	2519	0 263 11072 9
Poppy Girl	*Jacqueline Gilbert*	2520	0 263 11073 7
To Speak of Love	*Claudia Jameson*	2521	0 263 11074 5
A Man Possessed	*Penny Jordan*	2522	0 263 11075 3
Villa in the Sun	*Majorie Lewty*	2523	0 263 11076 1
At Daggers Drawn	*Margaret Mayo*	2524	0 263 11077 X
Land of Thunder	*Annabel Murray*	2525	0 263 11078 8
Boss of Yarrakina	*Valerie Parv*	2526	0 263 11079 6
The Last Barrier	*Edwina Shore*	2527	0 263 11080 X
One Life at a Time	*Natalie Spark*	2528	0 263 11081 8
So near, So Far	*Jessica Steele*	2529	0 263 11082 6
Girl in a Golden Bed	*Anne Weale*	2530	0 263 11083 4
The Final Price	*Patrica Wilson*	2531	0 263 11084 2

MASQUERADE HISTORICAL ROMANCE

The Country Cousins	*Dinah Dean*	M141	0 263 11121 0
Hostage of The Heart	*Linda Acaster*	M142	0 263 11122 9

DOCTOR NURSE ROMANCE

Sister Slater's Secret	*Holly North*	D59	0 263 11123 7
Flying Doctor	*Lilian Darcy*	D60	0 263 11124 5

LARGE PRINT

Matchmaker Nurse	*Betty Beaty*	106	0 263 11113 X
Yesterday's Shadow	*Helen Bianchin*	107	0 263 11112 1
Heaven Here On Earth	*Carole Mortimer*	108	0 263 11114 8